Quartet  Qrime

THE VERONA PASSAMEZZO

JAMES GOLLIN

The Verona Passamezzo

QUARTET QRIME

All of the characters in this book are fictitious, and any resemblance to actual persons, living or dead, is purely coincidental.

First published in Great Britain by Quartet Books Limited 1987
First published in the United States of America by
Doubleday & Company, Inc., Garden City, New York, 1985

British Library Cataloguing in Publication Data

Gollin, James
    The Verona passamezzo – (Quartet Qrime).
    I. Title
    813'.54 PS3557.0445

ISBN 0-7043-2646-9

Typeset by Reprotype Limited, Peterborough, Cambs
Printed and bound in Great Britain by
The Camelot Press plc
Southampton

for
Goldie and Isadore

Quartet  Crime

THE VERONA PASSAMEZZO

For to dance any Bace Dance, there behoveth
four paces, that is to wit: single, double,
reprise and braule.
                                    Robert Copland,
                  The Maner of Dancing Bace Dances (1521)

CHAPTER ONE

"Stop!" I ordered. Everybody stopped. Ralph sat back from the
keyboard, folded his arms across his chest and tucked his hands
in his armpits to keep his fingers warm. Outside, in the streets
and squares of Verona, it may have been sunny and hot, but here
in this ancient stone palazzo the damp and the cold spelled
March, not mid-May.

David turned his lute belly-up on his lap and checked the
joint between belly and neck to make sure the glue was holding.

Terry twiddled his fingers over the holes of his bass recorder.

Udo, our rented cellist, wearing his usual toothy grin, let his
bow skid carelessly across his open strings to show how tire-
some he found the proceedings. Then he too sat still.

Slowly, Sabrina let out her breath. "Now what have I done?"
she inquired in injured tones.

"That's an A natural," I said, "not an A sharp. You're hitting
it too hard, which is why it's coming out sharp."

"Well, Lord above," Sabrina said, "Professor Nehring says I
should always lean into a note."

"Who's Professor Nehring?" I asked.

"He's my expression teacher. At Augsburg."

"I thought you were studying with Madame Klagenhafer."

"I am, for production. She doesn't do expression. Madame
sends everybody to Professor Nehring for expression." Sabrina
used both hands to toss her long brown hair back over her
shoulders. She did it prettily. Sabrina did most things prettily.
She had obviously been voted the best-looking girl in her high
school senior class, and she had the technique to go with her

standing. Sabrina was fine to look at. She was a big girl, and singing had built up the muscles of her throat and chest. But she was no hypermammalian freak, and singing hadn't thickened her middle or turned her walk into a waddle.

As for Sabrina's pleasant young soprano, so far her teachers hadn't done anything too awful to it. But still, I was having my problems. Underneath her sweet girlish manner, Sabrina Englander had the stubbornness of a North Carolina mountain mule.

"Sabrina, listen to me," I said. "You're supposed to be a nymph. You know, kind of . . . disembodied." Sabrina looked pleased. "But you're not going to *sound* like a nymph," I went on severely, "if you nail that high A like Brünnhilde on her wedding night."

"Well, Alan, what do you want me to do?" Somehow, she gave my name three extra syllables.

"I want you to float that A, not lean into it."

"But Professor Nehring—"

"Professor Nehring isn't rehearsing you in this aria, I am."

"Once I am meeting this Professor Nehring," Udo the cellist said unexpectedly. "Professor Nehring is not singing anything earlier than *Tannhäuser*, I think."

"There, you see? No teacher can be an expert on everything," I said in my smoothest style. "Please. Try it my way. Just let it come, and think nymph."

Sabrina giggled. "I'll try," she promised. She put her feet together, straightened her back and took a couple of deep breaths, the way one of her singing teachers, probably her church choirmaster, had told her always to do. "Ready."

I nodded to David, Terry, Ralph and Udo.

For about the eleventh time that afternoon, lute, recorder, cello and harpsichord took up the languid eight bars that led into Sabrina's big first-act aria. And for the fiftieth time, I wondered how I'd ever gotten myself into the quagmire of coaching an untried soprano from Forest City, North Carolina, in a seventeenth-century opera about Bacchus, Ariadne and a posse of nymphs and shepherds on an island in the Aegean.

"*Ah! destino crudele* . . . ," Sabrina warbled dolefully. But I knew better than that. It wasn't cruel Destiny that had lured me to Verona, and Ralph, Terry, David and Jackie with me. It was plain old dirty money. The Festivale di Verona was one of the most solvent summer music festivals in Europe, and as the result of events that I'll sort out later, we were one of this summer's big attractions.

I should probably do *some* explaining right now, starting with the cast of characters. My name is Alan French. Ralph is Ralph Mitchell, Terry is Terry Monza, David is David Brodkey and Jackie is Jackie Craine. Collectively, we're the Antiqua Players. We've been going by that name for the past seven years—ever since we first got together in New York to specialize in performing early music on early musical instruments. Come to one of our concerts and you might find yourself listening to the suave sound of baroque flute, oboe, viola da gamba and harpsichord in a Telemann trio sonata. But we might also be playing more exotic instruments—krummhorns, sackbuts, the schryari, the musette—in a program of medieval Netherlandish dances. We like to move around in preclassical music, and we think we're good at adapting to the very different styles of different periods and at putting a professional patina on everything we play.

In the beginning, we were lucky to land an occasional booking in a church hall or a junior high auditorium. We've ridden buses through blizzards to the campuses of colleges you've never heard of, to play for audiences of seven or eight half-frozen faculty wives. Then, a hundred dollars was a big fee.

In those early days, we'd sometimes have to start our rehearsals at midnight, simply because most of us had other jobs and couldn't get away any earlier. I was one of the lucky ones. Thanks to my iron-willed mother, I play both flute and violin, and play them well enough to scratch out a living in music in New York. I've done everything from stints in musical-comedy pit orchestras to fill-ins at rock recording studios. And I teach, too.

I glanced around the room at the others. At Ralph, his eyes half closed as his right hand found ways to add zest to the figured bass. Ralph's got a trust fund, but his rage for buying and restoring antique harpsichords sucks up most of the income. Even now, when things are better and the Antiqua Players are almost prospering, Ralph hangs on to his job as an accompanist at the Barn, his name for a very fancy school of ballet on Central Park West.

David was sitting casually, echoing the bass line of the aria so gently that I could barely hear him. But I knew that if he stopped, I'd realize right away that something was missing. David's a little like the lute himself. He's quiet. And seductive. He claims that when he's not playing with us, he never does anything. It's certainly true that he brings out the maternal instinct in well-fixed young women, of whom he has a seemingly endless supply. But David has been seen at the bench in the shop of his ally, Jake the luthier, who acts as his pawnbroker and answering service. There's good money in stringed-instrument repair.

Terry may be the luckiest of us all. Terry's uncle owns Monza's, according to Terry the one and only gourmet Italian restaurant in all of Queens. When Terry's not practicing or playing, he works at Monza's. He's been a busboy, a waiter and an assistant night manager, and his uncle thinks he's got the right stuff to take over someday. Fortunately, the uncle is also a music lover, so Terry doesn't yet have to choose between his two vocations. And whenever he wants, he gets his lunches and dinners free.

Udo the rented cellist didn't count. He was only there because the fifth Antiqua Player couldn't be there. The fifth Antiqua Player is Jackie Craine.

Picture to yourself a tall, slender girl whose squarish face is framed by a fall of blue-black hair and whose arms and hands are as elegant as a dancer's. Now, add to the picture a personality miraculously free of the vagueness, deviousness, selfishness and cunning that grow on musicians like psychic acne. Jackie is never late for rehearsals. Rain or shine, she gets in her practice licks every day. She pays her bills on time, she remembers her baby nieces' birthdays and in general she runs her life like a grown-up.

If it weren't for two things (apart from her good looks, that is), Jackie Craine would be insufferable.

One of the things is that, musically, Jackie is a very shiny rising star. Her instrument is the viola da gamba, the cousin of the cello and a mainstay of our kind of music. The gamba is big, awkward and easy to play badly. Jackie plays it masterfully. Over the past couple of years, she has displaced an elderly Swiss virtuoso named Heinrich Wunschler as the best gamba player in the world. What's truly amazing about this is that Wunschler *adores* Jackie. Jackie Craine on gamba is part of why we're grabbing off more than our share of the available preclassical concert business.

The other thing about Jackie is that behind all of her talent, determination and polish is a small-town girl who can still get misty-eyed, and who sometimes even gets misty-eyed about yours truly.

As for me, I'm sure it hasn't escaped you that I am more than fond of Jackie Craine.

Just then, Sabrina put a rude end to my reveries about Jackie. She did this by reaching up for the high A we'd just been discussing, gulping in air and belting it out the way Barbra Streisand in full cry belts out "People who need PEE-pul!" It was horrendous.

I didn't have to bellow "*Hold it!*" the way I did. Ralph had already snatched his hands from the keyboard and put them over his ears. Terry blew a really ugly A on the recorder. David looked unhappy. Udo flipped his bow on the carpet.

"Oh, *shit,*" said Sabrina tensely. "I forgot." Face flushed, she flung herself into a chair. And before anybody else could say a word, the door opened and in walked Jackie, her arms full of bundles.

"I'm sorry," she said, "I'm interrupting."

"No you're not," I said. "In fact, you're just in time."

"I'm so *dumb,*" Sabrina said in accents of despair.

"Hey. Take it easy," Terry said soothingly. But nobody contradicted her.

Udo tilted his cello on its side and stood up. "I go now out for coffee," he announced.

"Fine," I said, "as long as you're back in five minutes."

"What's the problem?" Jackie asked. She began putting down her packages.

"I just can't *sing* this stupid part," Sabrina said loudly.

"Hey, Jackie," Terry said, "did you pick up any of that caccio-cavallo?"

Jackie laughed. "Of course," she said.

"It's driving me *crazy*," Sabrina said even more loudly.

Jackie turned to look at her. "What is?"

"This doggone aria. He wants me to throw away the high A—"

"Not throw it away," I said. "Float it."

"—and I *can't*."

"Wait a minute," Jackie said, eyeing me balefully. "Is he beating up on you?"

"Yes," said Sabrina. "I mean, no. Not on purpose, I mean, but yes, he is."

"Alan French, you should be ashamed of yourself," Jackie said.

"Why?" I inquired of the world. The world didn't answer.

"Show me the music, Sabrina," Jackie said. The two heads, one light-haired, one dark, bent over the part. "Okay. Now, where do you breathe?"

"Here," said Sabrina, pointing.

"Try breathing earlier," Jackie said. "Breathe *here*. After your breath, just keep moving, know what I mean?"

"What if I run out of air?"

"You won't," Jackie said matter-of-factly. "Try it. Ralph?"

"Sure." Ralph, Terry and David fed Sabrina the last four bars of her introduction. Midway through them, Udo came in, sat down, picked up his bow and joined in.

"*Ah! destino crudele* . . ." But all at once Sabrina was no longer laboring like the little engine that couldn't. Her voice was threading itself sweetly through the music. The shapes of the phrases, instead of being blurry with effort, were standing out distinctly. I waited for the high A. This time, because Sabrina hadn't filled up her lungs like a sponge diver before cutting loose, the A *did* float, and as if by magic the suspense I wanted materialized. Then Sabrina sang on unforcedly toward the final quiet cadence.

Udo beat his bow lightly against the cello in a gesture of applause. "*Ja, ja,* this was very good, I think."

"I think, too," I said.

"There!" Jackie said. "Of *course* you can do it."

"I can, can't I?" Sabrina said wonderingly.

"Don't forget to mark the place where you breathed," I said. With Sabrina, you had to strike while the iron was hot.

"I've got a pencil right here," said Jackie.

"Let's break now," I said, "and get back together around eight tonight."

As we were leaving the rehearsal room, a young man I'd never seen before approached Jackie. "Signora Craine?"

"Signorina," Jackie corrected him with a mischievous grin.

"*Ah, scusi.*" The young man smiled back. "The count presents his compliments," he went on in very good English. "He wants to know whether the *signorina* would wish to be driven to the airport. If so, the count will send his car at sixteen hours."

"Tell the count yes, and thank him," Jackie said.

"And I'll ride out with you," I said. "Three cheers for the count."

A cavalier may dance the pavan wearing
his cloak and sword . . . And the
damsels with demure mien, their eyes
lowered save to cast an occasional
glance of virginal modesty at the
onlookers . . .

Thoinot Arbeau,
Orchesographie (1589)

CHAPTER TWO

On the icy evening four months earlier when I'd first heard of
Count Emilio Sabinetti, I definitely hadn't felt like cheering. I
was still tired from the concert we'd played the Saturday before,
and I'd had to give a violin lesson late in the day. My pupil was
the exceptionally talented, exceptionally nasty eleven-year-old
daughter of a woman orthodontist. Her apartment is all the way
over on East End Avenue. My apartment is on Amsterdam.
That's a long crosstown bus trip for an exasperating experience.
"One of these fine days," I said to Jackie as I brushed wet snow
off my coat, "I'm going to give Vikki's mommy the chance to
practice on a whole bunch of her daughter's missing front
teeth."

"Now, now," said Jackie. "You know you love Vikki dearly."

"Only when she practices," I said, "and not always then.
What she needs—"

"I know. The whip. Well, you're not going to use it on *our*
kids. I won't let you."

"You're sadistic," I said.

Jackie put down her magazine and eyed me fondly. "You poor
thing," she said. "Out in the cold with your violin."

"Yes, and playing for pennies," I said, "while the rich people
go in and out of the door of the café and never even offer me a
cup of coffee."

"I know something better than coffee," Jackie said. She wriggled closer to me on the couch, put her arms around me and squeezed.

"Are we starting on those children right now?" I asked her. I began systematically kissing the triangle of white skin that showed at the base of her neck, above the collar of her sweater. I started in slow four-four time, switched to triplets and then to a kind of polka rhythm.

"You're driving me insane," Jackie muttered emphatically. She stopped me momentarily by twisting around until she could reach my mouth with her own. That was fun. It also put a lot of Jackie within easy reach of my fingertips.

"I like it when you wear a bra," I said when we came up for air.

"Would you mind repeating that?" Jackie said. "For the past five years, you've been telling me that you like it when I *don't* wear a bra, which I almost never do, because you made me get liberated."

"There is that aspect of it," I admitted. "But I enjoy figuring out the hooks."

"Gives you something to think about, you mean, while you're toying with me?"

"Um-m-m," I said.

"Well, you'll have to stop toying."

"Why?" I asked reasonably.

Jackie disentangled herself from me and sat upright. "Don't be angry," she said, leaning over to give me a final kiss. "But we have to get dressed. Terry's coming. And we're going out."

"Who says?"

"Tonight's the wine-tasting. You remember, Terry's friend."

"Oh, *no,*" I moaned. "You're sure it's tonight?"

"Positive. Now, get dressed. It'll be fun."

"Come on, Jackie," I protested. "It's freezing out . . ." But I didn't protest too much. Jackie works too hard, and sometimes I do, too, and we almost never go out in the evening to anything that isn't musical.

"It'll be over by ten," she said, "and we can come back and I'll cook you a delicious dinner."

"And after dinner?"

"You hurry up and get ready."

I did hurry. I hurried so much that I had to retie my necktie twice because the ends wouldn't come out even. Terry met us in the lobby and we hurried to the subway, where we naturally had to wait fifteen minutes for a train. By the time we made it to Le Cheval Vert on Fiftieth Street, Jackie was edgy, Terry was grumbling and I was out of breath. Predictably, New York being New York, everybody else was late, too.

"You see?" I said as we joined the damp crowd at the checkroom counter. "We didn't need to rush at all."

Jackie was wearing the new moss-green dress that was the real reason for going out. It fitted her like paint. When she thought nobody was watching, she stuck out her tongue at me. Terry laughed.

"Ah, Terry! And Alan and Jackie! Welcome!"

Terry's friend Diane was in cream-colored silk, several bright scarves, lipstick and perfume to match and quite a lot of chunky gold jewelry. Several weeks ago, Terry had brought Diane around to the studio. In one swooping sentence, Diane had announced that her job was building up the international wine trade—"I'm the one who *singlehandedly* did the boom in Australian whites"—and had commanded us to show up here tonight. "You *have* to come. I *need* you. And you'll be in on the ground floor of a *craze* for Nebbiolos."

Underneath the makeup and chutzpah, there was something sad-eyed and single about Diane that made it hard to say no. So Jackie and I surprised ourselves and said yes.

Diane took possession of us, marched us over to a table holding an army of bottles and thrust big cool glasses of white wine into our hands. "Terry, you're coming with me," she said. "There are some people I want you to meet." He shrugged agreeably. "Now, I'll be back in a minute," Diane said to us. "Be ready to tell me what you really think of the wine!" And away she went, legs pumping determinedly, scarves fluttering in her own breeze, with Terry in her wake.

I stood and sipped and watched, trying as if I were at a concert to size up the house. It wasn't a shy assemblage. People were pushing past us to get at the wine. One young man in a white suit, a deep orange shirt and a lemon tie elbowed me aside and smiled ingratiatingly at Jackie from under his eyebrow-pencil mustache. I gave him a baleful stare, which I'm happy to say made him mumble an apology and turn away.

"Oaf," Jackie said.

"He certainly is," I said.

"Not him," Jackie said ungrammatically. "You."

"I am your escort," I said. "It is my duty to see that you are spared the attentions of unprincipled strangers."

"You are being impossible," Jackie said. "Have some more wine and *try* to behave."

"I don't know what you think," I said, "but this wine-tasting thing doesn't seem very scientific. To me, it looks just like a cocktail party."

"Hello again, you two," said Diane, reappearing out of the mob. "Come and meet my favorite count."

"I don't want to meet any counts," I said. I was beginning to think of the subway ride home.

"But I want you to," Diane purred insistently. "He's a really, really terrific person. Besides, it's his wine you're gulping down."

The man at her side was clearly trying not to overhear this conversation. I had to sympathize, even though I had doubts about the man himself. He was wearing a dove-gray double-knit suit. It bore no resemblance at all to the double-knits you see on the salesmen in from Akron for the big convention. This suit was soft-textured, like finely woven chain mail. It fit to perfection. I resented the total absence of wrinkles, just as I resented the man's shirt, white with a thin *lilac* stripe, and his face, with a nose a shade too bold and a suntan that was an insult to hard-working New Yorkers mired in February.

"Count Emilio Sabinetti," Diane said with unction, "Jacqueline Craine and Alan French."

"How do you do?" Jackie said.

I grunted a greeting.

The count's face creased in a smile. "Ah," he said, "I have already met Mr. Monza. I am delighted to meet you. Since you are musicians, I will shake your hands very, very gently." The hand he held out looked as if it could easily crush black walnuts, but the grip, as promised, was gentle. "Miss Craine," the count said, "you make me want to behave exactly like a count in opera. To kiss your hand a little more vehemently than I should and tell you how beautiful you are."

Jackie flushed slightly, but she'd dealt with this sort of thing before. She bit her lip, lowered her eyes and fetched forth an enchanting smile. "One more word," she said, "and I'll fall fainting at your feet."

"Emilio, how come you never talk to me like that?" Diane demanded.

For one appalling instant, I was afraid the count was going to tell her. But he simply smiled and said lightly: "Diane, my dear, with us things are all business. Otherwise . . ." Then he turned to me and said, "But I am being outrageous."

"All part of the day's work," I said.

The count looked at me sharply. He laughed aloud. "You are right, it is useful. Like the title itself. But I must tell you, my friend, you are lucky in your companion."

Perfect suit or not, it was impossible not to like the man. "I know what you mean," I said.

"Take a little more wine, both of you," the count said, "and let me drink with you to your happiness. It is wine I made, after all, so it is quite safe to drink. Of course," he added deadpan, "you should boil it first. Like the water in New York."

"He's teasing you," said Diane, a note of exasperation in her voice. "Most Italian wine is pasteurized before it's blended. But not the count's wine."

"Hush, my dear," the count said. "No trade secrets." His eyes twinkling, he took a sip from his glass in response to his own toast. "Also, we should drink to our future relationship." He sipped again, and we drank with him. It was delicious wine. "You are wondering what sort of relationship I could be having with you. Well, I will tell you."

But Diane didn't give him the chance. "Now, Emilio," she said, "I warned you. This is a party to sell *wine*. You have to work with all the guests, not go off in a corner with just two of them."

The count nodded. "Okay, Diane, you are right, of course. Mix me!" We all laughed politely. But as Diane edged him away, he called back to us. "Please! Wait for me! I should like to talk more."

"I wonder what that's all about," I said.

"I can't imagine," said Jackie, "but I like the count."

I agreed with her. He might be a rich wine hustler and a public relations lady's dream, but Count Emilio was still a nice man. "Let's have some more of his wine," I said.

I joined the mob at the table, persuaded an overworked bartender to refill our glasses and juggled my way back through the throng. I wasn't a moment too soon. As I might have known would happen, the lad in the white suit and the lemon tie had moved right in.

". . . you play the gamba?" I heard him ask Jackie. He moved a few inches closer to her, which practically put him in her pocket, except that her dress had no room for pockets. "What's a gamba?"

"The gamba is a Central African percussion instrument," I interrupted. "Very primitive. The tribesmen make it out of the skeletons of their slaughtered enemies. Just the skulls and torsos, of course."

"I see," the young man said.

"The gamba is sounded by striking the dried bones of the upper body with the head of the femur, or thighbone," I went on in my best ethnomusicological manner. "Miss Craine here obtains quite a remarkable xylophone effect with a glissando along the rib cage."

"She does?" said the young man. He eyed Jackie rather anxiously.

"If you wish," I said, "Miss Craine will describe in detail how she makes gambas. You begin by removing the skin—"

"That's okay," said the young man, backing away. "I get the picture, really I do."

"I'm so glad," I said.

"Alan French, I could *murder* you," Jackie said after the young man had fled. "A glissando along the rib cage! Shame on you!"

"Sweetie," I said, "I only did it to prevent that dude from playing a glissando along *your* rib cage."

"Has it never occurred to you," Jackie asked frostily, "that I am perfectly capable of taking care of myself?"

"Sure it has," I said. "I was only looking after *his* interests."

Jackie looked crossly at me for a moment, then relented and blew me a kiss.

"Can't we go off somewhere?" I said.

"A wise idea, Mr. French. An excellent idea." It was the count, emerging glass in hand from the crush and walking us to a relatively unpopulated corner. "Let us take a moment to talk before my good friend the *signorina* Diane finds us."

"She's over with Terry," Jackie said, "and they're surrounded by a whole gang of people. I don't think she can see you from where she is."

"Good," said the count. "She is a remarkable person, but I have been in New York one whole week and I have done nothing but smile. My face is *tired* from so much smiling."

"Count Emilio," I said, "what do you want to talk about?"

"Music," said the count. "I want to talk about music. I was at your concert, you know."

"How nice!" Jackie said.

"You were?" I said, surprised.

"Oh, yes," said the count. "I liked it very much. *Very* much. You see, I am from Verona. You know Verona?"

"Not really," I said.

The count looked crestfallen. "Well, it is a city in the north of Italy," he began.

"That much I do know," I said, "and of course about Romeo and Juliet."

The count sighed.

"And that it's beautiful," Jackie added diplomatically.

"Okay, fine, very good," said the count. "Then you should also know that Verona is a very musical city."

"Isn't there a festival?" Jackie asked.

"*Bravo!*" said the count. "You are right. The Festivale di Verona, and this year I am *capo di comitato*—you would say, chairman." He made one of those indescribable Italian shaking-of-the-fingers gestures with the hand that wasn't holding the wine glass. "You understand, I am in the wine business in a serious way. Otherwise"—he made a wry face in the direction of Diane and her retinue—"otherwise I would not be over here *smiling* so much. But I am also serious about the arts. Not just because it is good for my business, although it *is* good, I admit. But because art is good in itself. This year, our *festivale* will be of the Renaissance."

I began to be more interested. People who sponsor Renaissance music festivals don't grow on trees.

"We are presenting an opera," continued the count. "*L'Arianna*, by Jacopo di Preti. You have heard of di Preti?"

I hadn't.

The count looked amused. "Of course not. If you had said otherwise, I would have been suspicious. But he is local, Veronese, a pupil of the great Claudio Monteverdi. So . . . we have engaged an artistic director, singers, a small orchestra, and they will do this opera."

"Very nice," I said.

"But we also have other opportunities for music. For vocal ensembles, *gruppi da camera*, everything. You are interested?"

"Fascinated," I said.

"You would consider performing?"

"When is this festival?" I asked.

"It takes place in the first two weeks of June. We would invite you to come earlier, to acclimatize yourselves, to rehearse—"

"To come much earlier would cost a lot of money." I was thinking of how much it does cost to feed and shelter musicians on tour. Even for a group our size, the expenses mount up alarmingly.

The count didn't bat an eyelash. "It is only for ten days or so. We would take good care of you, I assure you."

What the hell? If Count Emilio wasn't worrying about an extra five grand or so, who was I to unsettle his mind? "And the fee?"

"Fees are negotiated by the director. I only ask if you are interested. If you are, as I hope, then I will cable Verona and they will be in contact with you."

It sounded crazy. For obvious reasons, festival directors don't like festival sponsors to tell them which artists to hire. But when I said so to the count, he laughed. "That is no doubt the case in most festivals. But ours is different."

"At least let us send over a couple of tapes," I said.

"Later," said the count. He took out a neat little notebook and carefully wrote down my address and phone number. "You will hear from us very, very soon."

"That will be wonderful," I said, hoping my skepticism wasn't too naked.

"And now," the count said, "it appears that my little holiday with you is ending." I followed his glance across the room. He was right. Diane, her seminar on wines over, was heading purposefully in our direction.

"Emilio," she said with a reproachful look, "where have you been hiding?"

"All right, Diane," the count said, "right away, I'm coming." He took Jackie's hands in his own and smiled into her eyes. "*Cara mia*, your playing the other night gave me almost as much pleasure as your beautiful face. Please . . . prevail on your Mr. French to accept an engagement so that we may meet again—"

"Emilio!"

"—in more relaxed circumstances. Mr. French—"

"*E-mi-li-o!*"

"Goodbye, Count," I said.

"Until May!" the count exclaimed over his shoulder as Diane seized his arm and towed him away.

I shuddered. "Good God. I never knew what 'henpecked' meant until now."

"You see how lucky you are," Jackie said.

"Oh, sure," I said. "I get to be dragged out on a miserable night after a miserable day. I get to drink three glasses of white wine and hear all sorts of chatter—"

"And bully a harmless boy who was just trying to make conversation."

"That, too. And as my reward, I get to meet a count who heads the sucker list for some wingding in Verona—"

"You make it sound like a bar mitzvah celebration."

"For all I know, that's what it is."

"Gee," Jackie said. "I thought you liked the count."

"That's the funny thing," I said. "I do."

Jackie began to laugh. "I know what's wrong with you," she said. "Finish your wine and let's tell Terry. We're going home."

About ten o'clock the next morning, I was thumbing through the stack of bills on my desk and wondering idly which ones, if any, I could possibly afford to pay. Jackie was practicing. The silvery sound of her gamba was mixing itself up synesthetically with the smell of the coffee in the kitchen. There was even a cone of watery sunshine filtering through the grime on the studio windows. All in all, a plausible beginning for the day.

Crw-w-w-k!

Jackie's bow arm faltered momentarily, and I jumped in my chair. But we both know well enough what in the apartment squawks like a crow in extremis. I hurried into the kitchen and grabbed the intercom off its hook before it could send forth another death cry. "Hello? Hello?"

"Hiya, Mista French!" The voice of Ramon the super sounded breathless, as if he'd had to run to the lobby intercom from the basement. Ramon usually hangs out in the basement because he and his cousin Incarnacion have the home office of their used-auto-parts empire down there in the tenant storage bins, and Ramon likes to keep an eye on his inventory. And his cousin. "Package on the way up."

"Okay, Ramon," I said.

"You welcome."

At almost the same instant, the doorbell rang.

"Hey, Jackie," I called to her. "Come look at this."

The scrawny lad with the beret, the earphones, the bubble gum and the hand dolly was already halfway down the hall. He'd left behind on our doormat a wooden crate stamped with a fancy seal and marked in big red letters "PRODOTTO IN ITALIA." I lugged the crate inside. "I'll go grab a screwdriver."

"This will be better." Jackie handed me the small pry bar I'd bought in the fall, just after the building's painters had swarmed through the place and painted every one of my windows shut.

I wedged the pry under a corner of the lid and leaned on it carefully. Nothing happened.

"Want me to do it?" Jackie asked.

"Just because you were raised on a farm . . . ," I began. I didn't bother to finish. Instead, I leaned harder. The wood crunched. Then it gave way in a shower of splinters, revealing the nest of bottles inside.

"The sweet pet!" Jackie said. "Is there a note? There must be."

There was, taped to one end of the crate. "Here," I said. "See what sweet pet has to say."

" 'My dear Miss Craine and Mr. French,' " Jackie read aloud. " 'It was so delightful to meet you. This is the red wine of my estate, specially bottled and *not* boiled. Please enjoy it in the anticipation of our next meeting. With compliments, Emilio.' Alan, that *is* sweet."

"I wonder if the wine is any good," I said. "If it is, it probably means he's decided not to make us an offer."

Jackie gave me a dirty look. "You just stop being so cyn:cal," she said. "I'm tired of the way you always think the worst of everybody."

"I'm sorry," I said humbly. "I prostrate myself. The count is a wonderful human being. But still, let's get a corkscrew and find out how good the wine really is."

It was very good. And despite everything I'd said, the offer the Festivale di Verona cabled us that afternoon was even better. A flat fifteen grand, split it any way we liked, for two weeks of rehearsal and six performances, two as a group and four as part of the festival ensemble. Plus round-trip air fare, accommodations and expenses.

"Italy, huh?" said Terry when I read out the terms at rehearsal late that evening. "Sounds okay to me. I better tell my uncle I won't be around for the start of the wedding season."

"There's sentiment for you," Ralph said. "I've always heard how much Italians love their homeland."

"What do you want from me?" Terry said. "My homeland is Queens."

"Never mind," I said hurriedly. "Ralph, do you want to make the trip?"

"My dear man, you must be joking," Ralph said.

"Just thought I'd ask. David?"

"What?" David had that intense look on his face. It drives the ladies wild. Of course, experience has taught us that when David looks his most intense, he's probably thinking that it's time for something to eat.

"Do you want to fly with us to Italy?" I said patiently.

"Oh, yeah, naturally."

"Well," Jackie said after a few seconds. "I guess I'm the only one with a problem."

"Some problem," Terry said.

Jackie's problem, if you want to call it that, was that her agent, Ivor Rhys, had signed her up for a solo appearance in London on May 29.

The day Ivor had given her the news, we'd held a wild celebration, by which I mean we'd pulled out all the stops at Uncle Weng's and ordered a triple portion of Szechuan duckling to go with our ginger pork and hot-oil string beans. We were all a little giddy. This was the first breakthrough for Jackie—for any of us, really—into the high-powered world of the soloist. We'd kidded Jackie until she'd blushed about flying the Concorde with Previn and Perlman and the big-shot pianists and singers.

Now, it didn't seem so funny.

One thing I knew for certain. Without Jackie, we weren't going to be our brilliant best in Verona.

I thought for a moment. "Jackie, it's simple."

"What's simple about being in two places at the same time?"

"Call up Ivor Rhys and tell him they'll have to fly you to Verona a couple of times for rehearsals."

"Oh, fine," Jackie said, "and lose the booking, not to mention Ivor Rhys."

"You won't lose anything," I said. "How much can the plane fare from London be, a couple of hundred bucks? If they've already got you booked, they'll be glad to pick up the tab."

"I think you're meshugga," Jackie said. We all laughed.

"You talk Jewish like from downstate Illinois," David said.

"I'm not crazy at all," I said. "Try it. Call."

In the end, she did call, making faces at us to keep quiet while she pleaded her case with the great man. When she did explain matters, Ivor Rhys couldn't have been nicer. He phoned the London management right away and let them know that their brilliant gamba soloist was so much in demand that she'd have to be flown to Verona for two rehearsals the week before the twenty-ninth.

"They moaned and groaned," Rhys said when he called back. "But they were flattered, really. They'll pay for the flights."

"I told you so," I said. But inwardly, I heaved a deep sigh of relief.

Ivor Rhys handles Jackie, but not the Antiqua Players. Our bookings, such as they are, go through me. So next day I took a copy of the Verona agreement down to Mickey Weintraub. Mickey's our lawyer. He handles our contract paper work and sometimes, if he's in the mood, he gives me lessons in how to haggle. Mickey is the Jascha Heifetz of hagglers. Most of his clients are successful rock musicians, the kind who have to sink most of their income into shopping centers and oil wells. They're the ones who keep Mickey in Brioni suits and Bronzini neckties. What he makes from us barely buys him his socks, but Mickey doesn't care. He claims we add an indispensable touch of class to his practice. It could even be true.

I stood there in his office while he looked over the agreement.

"You want to sign *this?*" he asked, as if it were a loan form from the Mafia. "Baby, it's your funeral."

That meant it was okay. I signed it happily.

We started by writing to Verona about our schedule, the festival, our rooms and, needless to add, money. But writing took too long, and soon one or another of us was telephoning Verona almost daily.

"My phone bill looks like the Soviet defense budget," I complained. But nobody paid any attention until I chopped off fifty dollars a head from the pay for our February concert. The phoning stopped as if by magic.

February gave way to March, and March to April. Suddenly, the slush that neither Ramon the super nor any of his cousins had ever bothered to shovel away was gone. The window washers came. So did the first sparrows. Jackie was working furiously on her London program and the rest of us were working, less furiously, I must admit, on Verona. Then, one cloudy day, we packed up our instruments, our music and ourselves, piled into three cabs and bounced and rattled out to what my mother still calls Idlewild Airport. Eight hours and one stop later, in a blaze of sunshine and a melodious clamor of Italian, we landed in Milan and caught the train for fair Verona.

CHAPTER THREE

The car the count sent for us was no Rolls or Daimler, but
something a little less ostentatious, a dark blue Mercedes sedan.
The driver was the same smiling young man who had asked
earlier whether or not we wanted transportation. His name, he
told us, was Mauro. First, he helped Jackie load her suitcase, her
briefcase full of music and her gamba. Then he held the door for
her, waited for me to climb in beside her and took his place
behind the wheel.

As Italian cities go, Verona is relatively sedate. The traffic is
by no means as hellish as it is in Florence, for instance. But it's
bad enough. Until we were outside the center of town and heading west and south toward Somma Campagna and the small
airport, neither Jackie nor I was relaxed enough to lean back
against the glove-leather upholstery and pay attention to the
other.

"How are you feeling?" I asked her.

"It's weird," she said. "I don't really believe it's happening
after all these months."

"It's happening," I said, "tomorrow night at seven-thirty on
the stage of Wigmore Hall."

"Don't," Jackie said. "You're giving me a serious case of stage
fright. As you know darn well."

The car rocked on its suspension as Mauro pulled out to the
left to avoid an elderly truck laden with what looked like reeds
or straw. I used the opportunity to move closer to Jackie and put

my arm around her. "You know your stuff," I said. "That's half the battle. As *you* know darn well."

She laughed shakily. "Except for that Abel."

There wasn't much I could say. Karl Friedrich Abel was the son of Bach's friend Abel. Like the father, the son was a high-grade journeyman musician. And when Jackie began preparing for London, we both found out that Abel the younger had written a great deal of tuneful but appallingly difficult music for the viola da gamba. That, of course, was all Jackie needed to know. She tackled one of the Abel sonatas and got it mostly under control. But it was still at the stage where on a good night it sounded great and on an off night, well . . . "The quick movements are okay," I said.

"I know," Jackie said, "but the adagio's going to be the death of me."

"Jackie . . . ," I said.

"*Christus!*" Jackie said unhappily. "Why didn't I—"

"Absolutely. Stay back in New York and keep on teaching at Farmingville until all your little girls are suburban mothers themselves and you are their beloved old nanny who made them all appreciate music."

"But can I really do it?"

"Jackie, I think you can. I know you can. Only . . . I certainly wish I could be there. It's strange for me, too. Frustrating."

"Now, now," Jackie tried to joke. "None of that." I heard a muted laugh from Mauro in the driver's seat.

"You have a wicked mind," I said for him to hear. "I meant that it was frustrating not to be able to be with you. It's the first time since we met that I won't be somewhere in the vicinity when you play a big date."

"It's good for me, I suppose," Jackie said slowly. "But . . . oh, Alan, I'm terrified. I wish you were coming with me."

"For two cents, I'd get right on the plane," I said.

"You can't," she said with an unhappy smile. "You've got rehearsals of your own. You should be practicing the violin more. And then there's Sabrina."

"You think she's going to make it?" I asked.

"I think so. Provided you and that awful Udo don't bully the poor girl to death."

"I'll try to be nicer to her," I said. "But to wind up coaching a soprano, of all things."

"*Ah! destino crudele,*" Jackie sang. Then she said: "Alan, will you be thinking of me?"

"I'm thinking that it's time we ended this nonsense and fulfilled the expectations of our thousands upon thousands of fans—"

"—and tied the holy knot of matrimony."

I hugged her hard. "You wouldn't want me to get bored with waiting, would you? And go whoring after strange gods. Goddesses, I mean."

"Especially not goddesses from Forest City, North Carolina, I wouldn't," Jackie said feelingly.

"Well, then," I said.

"When I get back. After tomorrow. Then we'll decide."

"It's a deal," I said. "But it better be soon. I'm not getting any younger, you know."

"I'm not either," Jackie said. But she held my hand tight, and the tension she was under actually did make her look younger. Younger and more vulnerable, like a child on the way to the doctor. "I don't want you to *worry,*" she said almost fiercely.

"Yes you do," I said. "And I will."

We sat quietly for a moment. The car swooped down a long hill and across a rattling iron bridge. Mauro had to slow up to make the sharp bend on the far side of the bridge. Fishing off the edge of the bridge was a teenage boy with the beginnings of his first moustache. He waved at us. Lucky little bastard, I thought. You don't have to go to London to play the viol tomorrow night.

"My shoes," Jackie said suddenly.

"Come again," I said.

She had already unzipped her suitcase and begun burrowing inside. "They must be in here," she muttered. "I'm sure I packed them . . . I know I did, but . . . they're not here. Oh, *no.*" Her face puckered with woe.

"Wait a minute," I said, groping in the suitcase and pulling out a shoelike bundle in a plastic shopping bag. "Are these they?"

Jackie grabbed the bundle. "Oh, yes," she breathed. "Thank God. They're the ones I'm wearing tomorrow night."

By the time we got the shoes stuffed back in the suitcase and the suitcase zipped up again, we were nearly at the airport. Jackie turned to me, took my face in her hands and gave me a kiss. "I'm a real mess, aren't I?" she said.

"Well, I've seen you in better command of yourself, it's true," I said.

"Do you think I'm falling apart?"

"Nope," I said. "I think that when the time comes, you'll have all of this worked out of your system."

"*Christus,*" she said, "I hope so." Mauro pulled up in front of the Art Nouveau terminal and stopped the car by the main entrance. He paid no attention whatever to the no-parking sign. We all got out.

"You wish me to take the *valige* to the counter?" Mauro asked politely.

"I'd better manage these," Jackie said, taking possession of the gamba and her music. But Mauro insisted on carrying her suitcase into the terminal and fetching her ticket. When he came back, he looked impressed. "Two seats are reserved for the *signorina,*" he said. "Why?"

"One for me, one for her," Jackie smiled, patting the case of her gamba.

"*Ah, sì,*" Mauro said. "It's fragile, eh?"

"Right. How much time—?"

"The *signorina* has perhaps ten minutes."

"In that case—" I said.

"Yes, we'd better get going," Jackie said.

"Of course," said Mauro. "There is time. Here are the *signorina's* tickets and baggage receipts. You depart from *porta* D."

"Thank you," Jackie said politely.

The young man smiled. "And, *signorina,*" he said. "I could not help overhearing," he said. "So . . . permit me to wish you every success in your concert."

"Oh," said Jackie. "That's so nice. Thank you again!"

"Goodbye," Mauro said with dignity. "*Signor,* I will wait for you in the car."

"He did that beautifully," Jackie said as we made our way down the usual airport cinderblock corridor toward the security gate.

"He sure did," I said. "I wish I was that graceful."

"Now, listen," Jackie said, turning to me just before we reached the two burly *carabinieri* on guard at the gate. She set down her gamba carefully, propping it against her hip. Then she reached up to tweak my nose gently, and brushed my cheek with her hand. "I'm going to be gone for just three days. Remember . . . no trouble. I've got enough to worry about without wondering what you're up to."

"No trouble," I promised. "Just practicing and coaching Sabrina and rehearsing and maybe a swim—"

"Passengers for BEA flight 42," intoned the loudspeaker.

"Darling Alan—"

"Get out there and do your stuff," I said. "I'll be listening to every note."

"I love you," Jackie said.

"Me, too," I said.

"Say it," she whispered. "Please say it."

"I love you," I said. We kissed, she picked up her gamba, moved quickly through security, collected her gear and looked back once with a wave. Then she was lost in the crowd.

For a long moment, I felt desolate. Musicians bounce around a lot, I told myself unnecessarily, and the better they are, the more bouncing they do. It was true, but it still didn't make me any happier to see Jackie leave. Especially since I had a hunch that this wouldn't be the last time I'd be sending her on her way.

Despite my gloom, the sun was shining brightly in that surreal blue north Italian sky and blasting off the paintwork of the count's Mercedes.

"Perhaps the *signor* would care to sit in front?" said Mauro in a sympathetic voice. "It will be less lonely."

I laughed. "Signorina Craine will be back in a few days. And there's plenty to do for the festival."

"You are leading the music—the orchestra?"

"No," I said. "Emmanuel Gardi is the music director. I lead a small group, but I'm helping one of the singers."

"That must be very interesting," Mauro said politely. He swerved to avoid an enormous tanker truck that had suddenly slowed for a turn off the main road. "*Fesso,*" he said under his breath and added a few more choice epithets. "The wine carriers, *signor,*" he said. "They don't care about any other person on the road."

"Is that what that is?" I said. "I thought they were carrying gasoline—*essenza*, I mean—or chemicals."

Mauro laughed. "No, *signor,*" he said. "Wine is what is inside those tanks. Though some of it"—he laughed again—"you could call it chemicals."

"It's that bad?" I asked.

"*Signor,*" he said solemnly, "it is worse than that. Much worse. This is a famous place in the world, is it not, for wine?"

"Certainly is," I said.

"Why is it, then, that the wine you drink—not the expensive wine they serve the visitors but the wine you drink every day— tastes like something I will not repeat? And costs more and more money every year?"

"The cost, that's probably inflation," I said. "We have it, too. But the count's wine, that can't be bad?"

"Oh, no, no," Mauro said quickly, "not the count's wine. His wine is very good. He is very . . . very severe about the goodness. It is something that is known about the count, how he is severe. But some of those others"—his lip curled expressively— "it explains why so many people, in the cities especially, have changed to drink beer."

"I didn't know that," I said.

"It's true," Mauro said. "In Italy, where the wine is the drink of the land, the people have to drink beer."

We were nearing the outskirts of Verona, and Mauro had to concentrate on his driving, so our conversation lagged. My thoughts returned to Jackie. I tried some telepathy. Don't practice tonight, I adjured her via thought wave. Just soak in a hot tub and turn on the television and get in bed. And dream of me.

Mauro interrupted my reverie of *her*.

"I'm sorry," I said, "I wasn't listening."

"Has the *signor* been a musician for many years?"

"Since I was a little boy," I said. "But as a profession, for money, about twenty years. What about you? Do you like music?"

He grinned a little shamefacedly. "In honesty, not too much. The fine music, I mean. But I like rock."

"I do, too," I said.

"You do?" he said incredulously.

In fact, Italian rock music is irresistible. In style, it's about ten years behind American rock. But the Italians give it a characteristic lyrical twist. Sometimes it comes out funny and frantic. But sometimes Italian rock has a cockeyed, grand-opera majesty to it that I find beguiling. I had the radio in my room at the palazzo tuned to a rock station, a fact that did not endear me to the serious musicologist types among the festival performers.

Mauro was still marveling at my fondness for his favorite music when he edged the Mercedes down the Corso Sant'Anastasia and stopped in front of the palazzo. "You are not like some of the musicians I have met," he said, dropping the formal third-person mode of address. "They are more . . ."

"Orthodox," I supplied.

He broke into a grin. "*Sì!* Exactly."

I thanked him for being our chauffeur. It was obvious that whatever Mauro's duties were, driving us was more or less a favor. "And be sure to thank the count. It was very kind of him."

"It was my pleasure, *signor*. And I will tell the count."

Mauro drove the Mercedes away with very little of the bravura rightly associated with Italian drivers. I went in through the huge wooden double doors and past the booth of Orlando the majordomo. The courtyard of the palazzo was a good deal less imposing than its street façade. There was an octagonal fountain at its center, but the bowl of the fountain was empty. Its concrete was seamed and cracked, and the iron pipe that fed it was bone-dry. The rim of the bowl was comfortably wide, though, which made it a good place to perch and gossip during rehearsal breaks. This afternoon, no one was there, so I kept on going across the courtyard and in through the door at the far side. I climbed the grand staircase to the *piano nobile*, where the rehearsal studios and the dining room were located, and then attacked the considerably less grand staircases up to the fourth floor and the bedroom I shared with Jackie. There was an elevator, an elegant affair paneled in what looked like chestnut. But it moved slowly and creakily, and most of us preferred the exercise of climbing the stairs.

I was a little anxious about Jackie and a little depressed about not being in London for her concert. In about an hour, I'd have to start rehearsing with Sabrina again. Until then, all I wanted to do was kick off my shoes and stretch out on a bed. The last thing I expected to find in our room was a visitor. And the last visitor I expected to find was the person who was actually there, sitting in our one and only armchair and drawing contemplatively on a thin cigar.

"How delightful," I said when I saw him, even though alarm bells were tinkling faintly in my brain. "What brings you here, Count, and what can I do for you?"

"You can give me some advises, Mr. French," Count Emilio said seriously. "And perhaps some help."

CHAPTER FOUR

I'd seen the count half a dozen times since we'd arrived and settled down to work, but always briefly and never alone. He'd been present at the opening reception, of course, along with a dozen other festival patrons. And he'd dropped in on a couple of rehearsals, standing or sitting unobtrusively at the back of the room for a moment or two, then slipping away. Compared with other sponsors of other musical events at which we'd played, Count Emilio was a model figure. Which made his presence here all the more surprising.

"Advice, you mean?" I asked him. "Sure. I love to give advice. But what on earth—"

The count held up a hand. "My dear Mr. French, in one moment it will be clear why I am coming to you. But first, please let me apologize for this intrusion and let me tell you of my situation. Please?"

"By all means," I said. What else could I say? Besides, the count in his earnestness was making me more and more curious.

"Very good," he said. Then he paused, searching for the right words and for several seconds not finding them. At last, he drew a deep breath. "It's so absurd," he said with a deprecatory smile. "But . . . Mr. French, I am in love." He put a hand absently up to his face and gave his nose a tug. "You know what it is, do you not, to be in love?"

"I do," I said.

"It is not easy at the best of times."

"No," I agreed.

"And when you are a man of my age in love with someone much younger . . . then it is *impossible.*"

The count paused to draw again on his cigar. It had an aroma so delicious that I half regretted having given up smoking. It was also a wonderful prop. "Well, Mr. French," he continued, "the girl is at least of good family. Respectable. Very beautiful. And not stupid, thank God! But not someone, you understand, that it would be appropriate for me to think of marrying."

I nodded to show that I understood. Alan French, man of the world, that's me.

"We have been together quite often," the count said. "We have been . . . lovers. *Beh!* you will say, so what? In this day of the Pill, who cares?"

I could think of a lot of people who might care, and the count was right there to confirm my thoughts.

"This is not Rome," he said, and the sound of his voice left me in no doubt about what went on in the Eternal City. "We are provincial, it is true. Backwoodsmen, the English would call us. But we still have regard for a young girl's reputation. We are not debauchees."

Debauchees! I was still savoring the count's old-fashioned term for it when he leaned forward and gripped my wrist with his hand. "Mr. French," he said, "my friend and I have been discreet. But . . ." He stopped. Then he said abruptly, "I have a cousin. A cousin by marriage."

Oh-oh, I thought, here it comes.

Count Emilio sat upright again and let go of my wrist. "Attilio is his name," he said. He added sardonically, "and the name suits him. Since we were small children, Attilio has hated me. Perhaps it is because I am the heir and he is only the son of my mother's sister, who was married to the lawyer in Vicenza who looked after the rice estates. Perhaps it is other things. Attilio is a coward, and I"—he shrugged half apologetically—"in some ways I, too, am a coward, but not one like Attilio.

"Perhaps you have guessed, Mr. French, what this Attilio has done."

"I can imagine," I said.

"You are right!" said the count. "He has found out about Margherita. How, I do not know. And this is why I am coming to you."

"Wait a minute," I said. "I really don't—"

"He has demanded a meeting. *Demanded,* Attilio! He would never *dare* do such a thing in ordinary life." Again, the count leaned forward. "I know what has happened," he said with intensity. "*Her* relatives have found out. They want matters stopped. So they have gone to Attilio's wife, the so-elegant Luciana, to make her send Attilio to *me.*"

"But still—" I began.

"Now I will explain," said the count. "Attilio, as I said, is demanding a meeting. He is a reptile, you understand, but of the family. So I must meet with him. Tomorrow evening, we have decided, and we have set the place. It is our winery at Sant' Ambrogio."

"What's the problem, then?" I asked him.

"I have nothing to hide," the count said. "But I must have a witness to what is said between Attilio and me. An honorable man who will listen and say nothing. You see my difficulty. Who will render me this service? No one in my family, clearly. And no one of Verona, not even a dear friend. Oh, a friend would accompany me, no doubt of it. But when the friend learned of Margherita, he would disapprove. He would hide his feelings, but I would know. Attilio would know. And soon the tongues would begin to wag and the whole town would know that Count Emilio Sabinetti had been disporting himself with a young girl like one of those *vitelloni* in the Fellini films.

"This is why I come to you." The count paused, partly for dramatic effect and partly because his cigar had gone out. He took a gold DuPont lighter from his jacket pocket and relighted the cigar. Then he said, "You are a total, absolute stranger. You don't care whether I live or die, or what happens to the reptile Attilio. Or to my Margherita. In a few weeks, after the festival and after all of this mess is over, you will be leaving Verona for good. But you will know exactly what takes place, and Attilio

will know you know. So there will be no lies on his part. No
pretense that I have said things that were not said. Made prom-
ises that were not made."

The count stopped talking and I sat there thinking about his
story. The whole thing was so theatrical, so *operatic*, that it made
me want to giggle. The roguish count and the young girl. And
yet, it could be true. Parts of it, anyway. The business about
Cousin Attilio could well be gospel. I have relatives who bear
more than a faint resemblance to Attilio.

The count cleared his throat. "Mr. French," he said, "I know
how busy you are, how preoccupied with the music. If I thought
that this trivial affair of mine would *in any way*"—he wagged his
cigar to give the words greater emphasis—"interfere with your
work, I would withdraw at once. But what I am proposing is
merely a ride in an automobile to a town a few kilometers from
where we sit now and a few moments of your time at an interview. That and no more."

"But I don't speak Italian," I reminded him.

"That is no problem," he said. "Attilio speaks perfectly good
English."

Don't get into any trouble, Jackie had said.

"Please, Mr. French," said the count. He said it in a way that
suggested he was unused to asking anyone for a favor.

"Where is this town?" I asked.

"Sant' Ambrogio? Fifteen minutes from here by car, that is
all."

"And what time is your meeting?"

"It is for seven o'clock at the winery office. The men will have
gone home by then."

Seven. Jackie's concert was to begin at eight. "Count, I'm
sorry," I said. "I will be needed tomorrow evening. I don't see
how I can break away."

The count eyed me shrewdly. "You are expecting a call from
London, is that it?"

"Exactly," I said.

"No problem," said the count. "I will speak to the majordomo
and he will transfer the call to the winery office."

"You can do that?" I asked.

"Certainly," said the count. "Don't you have call forwarding in the States?"

"If you can really arrange it," I said slowly, "I can't see any reason not to go with you."

"Wonderful, Mr. French, wonderful!" the count exclaimed. "You will be rehearsing tomorrow until when?"

"We usually break off around six in the evening."

"Excellent! I will pick you up at six, we will do our errand with the insect Attilio and we will be back here by eight. I promise it!" The count sprang to his feet. "Mr. French, I knew I could rely on your aid. I am very grateful. It is one of the things I love about Americans. They are willing always to take extra trouble—"

"Just so I'm back here by eight-fifteen or so," I said. "I want to schedule an evening rehearsal."

"*Mio caro*, no problem," the count said. "It is no more of a trip than the little journey to the airport this afternoon."

"By the way, thank you for that," I said. "It made life very much easier."

"I am happy it did," the count said at the door. "I will see you, then, tomorrow at eighteen hours. *Arrivederlà!*" And he was gone.

"If you ask me, dear heart," Ralph said at dinner, "I think you are definitely out of your mind. You've got *us* to rehearse and Sabrina to coach and Jackie to worry about and Manny Gardi on your back, and we've got to *do* this thing in a couple of weeks. But"—he shrugged—"if you want to give *il padrone* a hand, go ahead."

I managed to corner David just before rehearsal. His reaction was a little more positive. "Sure. Anybody can have trouble with a chick. Why should the count be any different? I can relate to going out there with him. You want me to come, too?"

I laughed. "I don't think so," I said, "but I'll give you a blow-by-blow when I get back."

Only Terry gave me a hard time. "Definitely no," he said

when I asked him. "Don't do it, don't have anything to do with it."

"What's the problem?" I said.

"Hey. I'm not much of a *goomba*," he said. "I barely speak a word of Italian anymore. But one thing I gotta tell you. Don't mess with anything to do with women. Not in Napoli, not in Verona. You start fooling around with that, you're gonna be in the deep minestrone, you dig it?"

"I guess so," I said. I tried to keep my voice noncommittal, but Terry was much too alert.

"Hey," he said again. "Have you already gone and told the guy you'd do this with him? Don't bullshit me, now. You have, right?"

"I have," I admitted.

"Christ almighty," Terry said. "If you and Jackie don't get married pretty quick, I don't know what the hell's gonna happen to you. She's the only one who can keep you out of trouble."

"Just tell me one thing, wise guy," I said. "Why don't you follow your own advice?"

"Huh? What the hell are you talking about?" Terry said, startled and ready to get angry.

"Wasps," I said. "Don't ever go messing around with anything to do with their women."

He looked at me hard for a second, then laughed. "I give up," he said. "Whatever you have to do, go ahead and do it."

Jackie called about midnight. She'd landed safely, gone to her hotel, called her accompanist to set up a run-through for the next afternoon, pressed her dress and gone out to dinner with the young man from the management firm handling the concert.

"You're meeting too many good-looking young guys," I said. "First Mauro, now this Reginald or Guy or whatever his name is."

"Guy is the *harpsichordist*, silly," Jackie said. "He's charming, and I feel very secure with him."

"I don't," I said, and we both laughed.

"Michael is the agent," she went on, "and he's charming, too.

"Pardon me for being mercenary," I said, "but how are ticket sales?"

"Not so charming," Jackie said, and we laughed again. "Michael didn't want to tell me, but I made him. They've got about half the house sold. About nine hundred tickets."

"Not too bad," I said. "What else?"

There was a lot else. Michael the agent had scheduled an interview on the BBC Third Programme morning feature show. She'd been invited to supper after the concert by the countertenor who was, as Jackie put it, Mr. Early Music in Britain. "Should I go?" she wanted to know.

"Of course, go," I said. "If I can't be there, Erick Pritchard is the one person you should be with."

"Alan." Her voice was suddenly subdued. "I think I should practice tonight. Just the Abel."

"God*damm*it," I started to say. But then I thought, what right have you got to yell at her? She's the one who's really feeling the heat. "Jackie," I said, "if you feel you should practice, go ahead and practice. But it's late, and you've had a long day. Don't you think you'd do better in the morning?"

She actually giggled. "You sound just like my mother," she said.

"All *right*," I said loudly. "That's *it*. I absolutely *forbid* you to take out your gamba. You get right to bed."

Jackie giggled again. "Now you sound like my uncle Colvin."

"Your uncle who?"

"Colvin. The uncle who ran the farm. Daddy was the meek and mild one. Uncle Colvin was *fierce*. He wouldn't let me practice when I was learning cello. He said it kept the cows and pigs awake."

"Well, I'm not like your uncle Colvin," I said. "I couldn't care less about the cows and pigs. It's *you* the practicing is going to keep awake. And I think you need your rest."

"You're sweet," Jackie said softly.

Then and there, I should have told her about the count's visit and his odd request. But I was trying to help her relax and it seemed to be working and I thought to myself, better not dis-

turb her with anything. "I'm not sweet at all," I said. "I'm
thinking in cold-blooded commercial terms. If you're not rested,
you might give a rotten performance, and my years of investment in you will be wasted."

"No they won't," Jackie said, even more softly than before.

"I guess not," I said.

"This is costing a *fortune,*" Jackie said suddenly.

"I love you," I said.

"It's still costing a fortune."

"Okay," I said, "let's say good night."

"No," she protested.

I made her promise not to practice for more than fifteen minutes. Then, I told her I loved her seven or eight more times. And
then, we did say good night.

About four in the morning, something woke me up. An unfa-
miliar sound. I lay in bed, wondering groggily what it was.
Then I realized. For the first time since we'd arrived in Verona,
it was raining. I rolled over and let the soft drumfire of the rain
lull me back to sleep.

When I got out of bed at eight-thirty, it was still raining.

"*Fa brutto tempo,*" said the majordomo, shaking his head, as I
went past him on my way out to buy a tube of toothpaste and a
Paris *Herald Tribune.*

"*Fa brutto tempo,*" said the lady behind the counter at the phar-
macy.

"*Sì,*" I mumbled, hiding my rudimentary Italian behind a
grunt for the hundredth time.

It stayed foul all day. Not quite cold enough for us to ask
them for heat in the rehearsal rooms—assuming that there was
any heat to turn on—but chilly enough to make it hard to concentrate on the notes.

By lunchtime, we had worked our way through our own material. The afternoon we spent on the ensemble pieces we were
playing with Emmanuel Gardi's chamber orchestra. The other
people in the orchestra were good, but this was only our second
full rehearsal and we sounded ragged. Manny Gardi was fight-
ing a virus. When he wasn't fumbling with the pages of his

score, he was using a very large handkerchief on his very red
nose.

By six o'clock, Manny was ready for a hot bath and bed, and
the rest of us were delighted to call it a day.

I half expected to see Mauro waiting with the car near the
front entrance of the Palazzo Sabinetti. But the count himself
waved a hand from behind the wheel of the blue Mercedes.
Luckily, I'd brought a lightweight raincoat with me to Italy.
Unluckily, I'd packed neither boots nor an umbrella. Who
thinks about umbrellas in Verona in May?

I sloshed across the muddy cobbles and climbed into the car,
grateful for the warmth of the heater.

"I have spoken to my people about forwarding any calls to the
winery," the count said as he eased the car past a fast-moving
trolleybus into the left lane. I shivered, not from cold. But the
count's lips didn't even tighten as he whipped us across the
Pietra bridge, past San Giorgio Maggiore with its Tintoretto
Baptism of Christ and a lot of other art I hadn't had time to see—
and might not ever see if the count didn't slow down—and out
of Verona on the road northward to Caprino.

"I appreciate your forwarding the call," I said as soon as I
thought it was safe to talk.

"Not at all," the count said. "It is you who are doing me the
favor." Without slackening speed, he cut into the right lane to
avoid a farm truck making a left turn. A few seconds later, we
were within about six feet of another truck. The count flashed
his lights and sounded his horn unavailingly. Before I could
cower down in the footwell, he was in the passing lane, around
the truck and back again safely. The count was making Mauro
seem like one of those elderly ladies who only drive to church
on Sundays.

"Have you heard from Margherita?" I asked, just to keep the
conversation going and my nerves quiet.

"Margherita?" said the count distractedly. "Er . . . oh, yes,
of course. Last night. She is very sweet." He stopped talking and
gripped the wheel in a way that plainly signaled the end of our
conversation.

I was reduced to looking out at the scenery, which consisted mainly of sheets of windblown rain and roadside buildings a lot like those you find in upstate New York. From time to time, I spotted what looked like commuter trains on the tracks that paralleled the road. Beyond the railroad and the Adige was a dimly seen agricultural landscape, sweeping upward along the slopes of the dun-colored hills.

I suppose I expected the count's winery to be a collection of wooden sheds and barns, with the vineyards themselves in the background. So I was vaguely disappointed when we swung off the main road, climbed a steep hill into the streets of a modern town and stopped in front of a low brick building that could have been an ice-cream factory.

"It's not very glamorous, eh?" said the count humorously.

"No," I said.

"No matter," the count said, "it's efficient, and that's what counts." He took keys from his pocket and unlocked the heavy glass doors. "We're early," he said. "The staff have gone home, and Attilio is not here. As long as we have a few moments, would you like to see the place?"

Never having toured a winery before, I was mildly curious. Besides, what else was there to do? "Sure," I said, "but will we hear the telephone if it rings?"

"Oh, yes," said the count. He stepped inside an empty office. "I've turned on the intercom. Now we'll hear it everywhere. Come this way." He walked me past the offices and down a corridor. The double swinging doors at the end led into a huge, dim, cement-floored chamber. "Prefab," the count said. "Not expensive." He flicked on switches and the room was flooded with light. At intervals along a central aisle stood big stainless-steel vats, linked by complicated systems of shiny steel and vividly colored plastic piping. The place looked like a miniature tank farm and smelled, ever so faintly, of fermentation and fruit.

"Where does your grandmother tread on the grapes?" I asked.

The count laughed. "The main press is there," he said, gesturing to a squared-off structure in one corner. "Come and take a look." We climbed steel factory stairs to a catwalk about

twenty feet above the floor. Our footsteps echoed noisily in the
deserted plant. The count pointed out the conveyor belt that
carried up plastic baskets of grapes for dumping into a huge
hopper. "In the old days, it used to take forty men to load the
press," he said. "Now we can do it with four or five." When the
hopper was full, its contents would be fed into the vat below
and the press turned on and allowed to squeeze the juice from
the grapes. "All automatic, you understand. You can see it best
from here."

We stood side by side on the catwalk to look down into the
glittering tub below. Even I knew that at this time of the year it
would be empty.

It wasn't.

The body lay facedown on the floor of the press, legs spread-
eagled, one arm flung above the head. It looked almost posed, as
if for some strange high-tech fashion illustration. Blood, quite a
lot of it, was puddled alongside the body and mirrored redly on
the steel walls and floor.

The count made an indescribable sound.

I felt the sweat break out on my brow. "Attilio?" I asked
unnecessarily.

"Sì," the count said. "I will go down."

"Better not," I said. "I'm sure he's—"

"He is my cousin," the count said. "I must."

Across from where we were standing, a wooden ladder was
clamped to a supporting stanchion. The count ran to slip it free,
lowered it into the press and climbed quickly down. Keeping
clear of the blood, he knelt beside the body and reached for a
pulse. Then he rose to his feet, shaking his head. I saw his hand
move as he crossed himself. He climbed back up the ladder. His
face was ashen. "Mr. French," he said as if he wanted to start
explaining something. But then he checked himself and went on
simply, "Come with me. We must call the authorities."

[M]y master, Misser Domenichino, showed
irrefutable judgment when he said that dancing,
particularly in the slow measure,
must continue to appear as an illusive shadow . . .

Antonio Cornazano,
The Art of Dancing (1455)

CHAPTER FIVE

We went into one of the offices to call. The count's Italian was far too rapid for me to follow, but he was obviously saying the right things. I simply sat down on a metal chair and stared out the rain-streaked office window, too shocked to react. It couldn't have been more than three minutes before a dark blue Alfa Romeo sedan slid smoothly to a halt behind the count's Mercedes. I watched numbly while the doors opened. Three plainclothesmen got out.

The count grunted something and went off to greet them at the winery entrance.

At the back of my mind, I was wondering what to say to Jackie when she called from London. Hi, honey, how was the concert, I'm a little tied up with a murder? Somehow, that didn't quite ring true, but I wasn't thinking too clearly and I just couldn't make myself come up with something different.

A rumble of voices and footsteps sounded in the hallway. The count came back into the office. He was followed by a man wearing a nondescript black nylon raincoat and, incongruously, one of those loden green German hunting hats with tiny narrow brims.

I stood up.

"Mr. French," the count said in English, "I would like you to meet Commissario Ratner of the Pubblica Sicurezza. He will be in charge of investigating this happening."

The commissario perched casually on the edge of a desk, took off his absurd hat and twisted it absently in his hands. He gave

me a small, tight smile. "You are American, Mr. French?" he
asked in accented but fluent English.

I said yes.

"And you are a friend of His Excellency's? Of the count's?"

I began to explain, but the count cut me off. From the word or
two I could understand, he was explaining my status. Finally, he
paused. The commissario nodded.

"You are a musician?" he asked me.

"That's right."

"You are playing in the *festivale?*"

"Yes."

"And you are residing where?"

Once more, the count interrupted. This time, I caught the
phrases that told the commissario I was an honored guest at the
count's own palazzo in Verona. The commissario listened. I
don't think I've ever seen *anyone* listen more attentively. He
waited patiently for the count to finish. Then he turned to me
again.

"His Excellency says that your young lady is away for a little
time and that you seemed lonely. So he invited you to dine with
him and his . . . *cugino?*"

"His cousin, yes."

"Did you know His Excellency's cousin before?"

"No," I said, "of course not. I never met him. I never even *saw*
him until . . . we found him tonight."

The commissario nodded. Then he said: "Mr. French, I want
you to think very carefully about your coming here to this place.
When you came, did you see any cars moving in the street?"

Instinctively, I looked outside. A lot had happened since the
commissario's arrival. There were now three dark blue police
cars parked outside, plus a Fiat ambulance. A small crowd had
gathered. A couple of uniformed cops, their short slickers shiny
with rain, had set up barriers to keep the entrance clear.

The commissario was waiting politely.

"I don't know," I said. "I don't think so. I remember thinking
when we pulled up how easy it is to park in this town."

The commissario smiled sourly. "Not in the *centro*," he said, "and not in the mornings. But that is of no consequence. You say you do not remember seeing any other cars here?"

"No," I said.

"Very well. Now, please consider. Were there any unusual events that occurred during your journey from Verona?"

"None," I said. "I did think Count Emilio was driving too fast."

Commissario Ratner smiled again, not quite so biliously. "You are not alone in that opinion." He put a forefinger in the crown of his hat and twirled the hat around a couple of times. As soon as he saw me looking, he stopped, embarrassed. "*E poi.* You accompanied the count from his car directly into the building?"

I nodded.

"And you saw and heard?"

"Nothing out of the way," I said. "Of course, our footsteps made quite a lot of noise."

"So that you would not of necessity have heard the steps of anyone making . . . a getaway." The commissario brought out the word with a certain amount of pride.

"That's right," I said.

"To summarize, then, you did not know the victim, you were invited casually to dine with him, you saw nothing unexpected on the way to this place, you saw or heard nothing unusual while you were here until you and the count discovered the cadaver."

"Exactly," I said.

The commissario sighed. "Very well, Mr. French," he said. "I will ask you to remain in this place while we finish our preliminary investigations of the scene and of the victim. We may have other questions to ask you. Later, if the outcome proves satisfactory, we will be able to release you from custody."

"Custody?" I could feel my heart start to pound. "Am I under arrest?"

The commissario looked a little apologetic. "Not technically," he said. "It is only a matter of convenience for us. It would not look good if we had the murderer in our hands, eh, and we let him get away? So . . . we will ask you to stay here."

At this point, the count burst out in Italian. I hoped he was telling the commissario that he was several kinds of fool for insulting an innocent American while the real murderer was several million miles away.

Commissario Ratner listened impassively. At length, he shrugged and said something terse in Italian. The count subsided, and the commissario then switched back to English. "We will be as quick as possible," he said.

"But I have a rehearsal," I said.

"At what hour?"

"Eight-fifteen. I mean, twenty-fifteen."

The commissario looked at his watch, a handsome affair on a gold wristband. "I am sorry," he said, "you will have to postpone. One of my men will telephone."

I asked him to ask Ralph to fill in for me, and he said he would. "And I am expecting a telephone call," I added, "from London."

"A call?"

"From my fiancée, who is performing there tonight," I said.

"She will call here?"

I looked at the count, who nodded and explained.

"Very good," said the commissario. "You may receive the call. Bernardo!" A younger version of the commissario appeared in the doorway. He and the commissario exchanged a few sentences. "Gentlemen, my associate Bernardo will remain with you while I check on the progress of the investigation. If you will excuse me . . ."

The next couple of hours were like every boring wait I'd ever experienced, with homicide as an added attraction. At one point, Officer Bernardo rose to his feet, smiled politely and left the room. I started to say something, but the count immediately put a finger to his lips to silence me, so I shut up. There was nothing to read, not even an industrial catalogue or a vintners' trade magazine in Italian.

To make matters worse, the telephone stayed quiet. My watch told me that Jackie's concert had begun, had reached intermission, had ended. No call. All right, I said to myself, she's playing nine encores. I gave her time for nine *long* encores. Still nothing. My mind kept hopping back and forth from Jackie to Attilio, until I was too tired to think. I must have dozed off in my chair, because the shuffle of footsteps in the corridor made me sit up with a start. The footsteps passed our door. Then came a blur of light through the office window. Aching with fatigue and tension, I peered out in time to see them load a long, bulky sack into the ambulance.

Count Emilio, standing at my side, quietly crossed himself.

That's when the phone decided to ring.

"Darling? Is that you?" Jackie's voice had that out-of-this-world quality you get when the call is via satellite. But there was more to it than satellites. In the background, I could hear excited voices, music and what sounded suspiciously like the clinking of glasses.

"It's me," I said.

"Well, where are you?" Jackie asked. "You're not at the palazzo."

"Never mind," I said. "How did it go?"

"It went—" I couldn't hear the last part of the sentence because of a hailstorm of squeaks and ghostly woodwind noises, presumably from outer space.

"What?"

". . . was fabulous," Jackie said, her voice suddenly as clear as if she'd been standing next to me. "The reviews won't be in until later, but I"—again the barrage of messages from Mars.

"Sounds great," I said. "Listen—"

"Darling, I have to run. They're giving me a party!"

"I can hear," I said.

"How are you?" Jackie said.

"Okay," I said. "Absolutely fine. Congratulations. But—"

"I'll call you later, when I get back to the hotel."

I gave up, told her I loved her and said goodbye.

Five minutes later, Commissario Ratner came back into the office. "I am sorry you were detained for so long," he said, "but we have had to make our preliminary investigation. You are free

to go now. But of course you will not change your residence
without notifying us. We will contact you tomorrow. There will
be a *deposizione* to sign, and as it is so late we have no clerk to
type it." He smiled his controlled smile. "So . . . tomorrow."

"Have you any idea what happened?" I asked.

The smile stayed on his face. It was neither friendly nor unfriendly. "So far, no," he said.

"Okay," I said to Count Emilio half an hour later. "What's
really going on? To begin with, there isn't any Margherita, is
there?"

The count sighed. His fingers bowled an olive around on his
plate. We were in the dining room of his club, a cavernous,
almost deserted refuge on the Lungadige Re Teodorico. To my
embarrassment, I was famished. I had more than done justice to
the huge platter of cold meats and the enormous mixed salad the
waiter had set before us, along with a bottle of red wine from
the count's own domains. Now I sat back in my leather armchair, sipped the wine and waited for the count to respond.

"No," he murmured at last. "There is no Margherita. She is
. . . a creation." He grimaced ruefully. "I wish she were the
reality. The reality is, oh, a hundred, maybe a thousand times
worse than a girl with whom one's affair has been discovered."

"It sounds pretty bad," I said.

Count Emilio stared at me. "My friend, I owe you the truth,"
he said. "But to tell you the truth may not be doing you any
favor."

Since there was nothing to say to this, I said nothing.

The count heaved another sigh. "The truth has to do with
money," he said shortly. He waved a hand and our waiter hurried over. He carried a silver tray on which reposed two of the
count's special cigars. "You will smoke?" asked the count, taking
one.

I shook my head.

The count nodded his thanks to the waiter, then went slowly
through the ritual with his little silver guillotine and a wooden
match from the container on the table. "Money," he repeated

with emphasis as the fragrance of the smoke drifted toward me like essence of hundred-dollar-bill.

I waited politely, as I knew I was supposed to do.

"Mr. French, we have held our lands north of Verona for eleven hundred years. Since before the year one thousand. My uncle, before he died, liked to claim that except for the Harsányis—Hungarians, nationalized now of course—we were the oldest landowning family in Europe. It's absurd, of course"— the count made a proud, deprecating gesture with his cigar— "but, still . . ."

On cue, I nodded encouragement.

"To be a landowner these days is a terrible burden," the count said sadly. "Taxes, inflation, repairs. And one's obligations to one's farmers. And the community. Terrible."

I tried to look sympathetic.

"I have mortgages on my properties," said the count shamefacedly. "We all have borrowed from those vultures in Milan. I less than some others. Even so . . ." He shrugged. "This is why I am so greedy to sell wine, why I come to New York. I need the money to pay the bankers. I need a great amount of money."

"I understand," I said. "But what's that got to do with—"

"Please listen." The count put a hand to his forehead in a gesture of fatigue, and I suddenly realized how much tension lay behind his *politesse*. "For two, three years, my wine sales were excellent. I made money, enough for the bankers and for me, too. I borrowed more to build the winery, but the winery is no problem. It makes money. The problem was last year's harvest."

"A bad year?" I asked.

"No, no," the count said. "A splendid year. In fact, an incredible year."

"I don't understand," I said.

"There was too much wine," the count said simply, "too much wine."

"Oh."

"Prices fell. Naturally they fell. So much good wine, and nobody was buying. They were all waiting, you see, the *vinaii*, the merchants, until we *had* to sell."

"So you got a bad price for your wine?"

"Oh, no," the count said. "My wine always sells for a good price." He explained then that he only bottled a fraction of the wine his vineyards produced. The rest he sold to wine merchants or wholesalers, middlemen who bottled the wine and resold it for export.

"I don't understand," I said again. "If you got such a great price for your wine, why are you in trouble?"

"I sell it in Marseille to some people, they will put it in a beautiful bottle with engraved label, *molto elegante*, and it will be vintage wine, *appellation controllée.*"

Light was beginning to dawn, or at least I thought it was. "You mean . . . these people are going to say your wine is fancy French wine?"

The count nodded.

"But isn't that against the law?" I blurted.

The count smiled. "Maybe," he said. "In France, it is not lawful to sell wine this way, I assure you. But for me to sell to some Frenchmen . . . how do I know what they will do with my wine after delivery?"

What the hell, I thought, it makes sense. "All right, but I still don't see why you're in trouble, or what it has to do with Attilio. Or me."

The count looked at me speculatively for a long time. Then he said, "Perhaps you are right, my friend. Perhaps I am imagining my problem. Perhaps I have no problem." He was still smiling, but the smile was more like a grimace of pain. It was patently obvious that he had more to tell and had made up his mind not to tell it.

"Except Attilio, of course," I said.

"Of course." The count looked at me bleakly. "As I said, he is . . . he was . . . of the family. He had found out something. About the wine. I do not know what, or how. Tonight, I thought I would find out what he knew. I know what he *wanted.*"

"What?"

"Money, certainly. But also, to have the power over me. What

I told you the other night was true. Attilio hated me and had envy of me. Such power would have meant much to him."

I looked across the table at the count. The jacket of his elegant suit was slightly rumpled, the knot of his tie not quite centered in the collar of his shirt. Exhaustion and strain had robbed him of some of his authority. His fine hands moved nervously, crumpling the linen of his napkin. I wondered if I believed him this time.

"You are angry," Count Emilio said as we got to our feet, "and I do not blame you. You are caught up in a minestrone not of your own making."

Hours earlier, Terry had used the same word to say the same thing. Why hadn't I listened?

The count said nothing more until we had left the club and were gliding in the blue Mercedes through dim narrow streets toward the palazzo. Then, staring straight ahead, he said, "Whatever happens, please believe that it was not I who killed my cousin. On my honor, I swear it."

This pair is excellent for making a tremendous
noise, such as is required at village fetes . . .
Arbeau,
Orchesographie

CHAPTER SIX

Jackie didn't call back until one o'clock in the morning London
time, which was two o'clock in the morning in Verona. After a
drumfire of comments ranging from "Yuck, how horrible!" (Sabrina) to "Hey. What did I tell you?" (Terry), everybody else
had long since gone off to bed. And edgy as I was, I had fallen
into an uneasy doze in the chair by the telephone.

"*Pronto,*" I said groggily, just in case the party at the other end
of the line wasn't Jackie Craine.

"Alan?"

"Unh."

"I'm sorry it's so late, but I'm back at the hotel now and
everything was wonderful. The Abel, the adagio, everything.
Alan, the reviews!"

"Good, huh?"

"I can't believe them. I'll bring all the papers. I can't wait to
see you. And Erick"—the hotshot countertenor—"was just darling."

"Jackie . . ."

"What's wrong?" My beloved has ears in the back of her head.

As quickly as I could, I told her. I could picture her sitting
there as she listened, her face serious, her free hand brushing
back a strand of hair. I hated spoiling her big night, and I told
her so.

"Don't be silly," she said. "You didn't mess it up while it was
happening, and there are lots of other good things I haven't even
told you yet. And I don't care how awful he was or what he was
doing, that poor man is dead."

"That's right," I said. "It's crazy."

"Are you sure you're okay?"

I drew a deep breath. "I am now. A lot better, anyway." It was true. I wasn't seeing all that blood trickle on the floor of the wine vat and listening to the sound Commissario Ratner's hat made as he twirled it on his finger. "I just wish it would all go away."

"I wish I could make it go away," Jackie said.

"Tomorrow night," I said. I made myself sit up straighter and change the subject. "Tell me about after the concert," I said. I was sure my voice was absolutely matter-of-fact, free of innuendo and of even a hint of jealousy, professional or personal.

Jackie laughed. "Well. Erick took me out to supper. At the Ivy."

"Hmph," I said. "Did he make a play for you?"

"If I say no, you won't believe me, and if I say yes, you'll be jealous."

"You're right," I admitted. "Did he?"

"Mostly he talked about music and Cambridge. He went to Cambridge, you know. And yes, he did. He made a mild attempt to get me to go home with him. He had some wonderful brandy he thought I should sample."

"And?"

"I told him I had to go back to the hotel and write out a six-part fugue in North German viol tablature. That stopped him."

It was my turn to laugh.

"Guess what else?" Jackie said.

"I'm afraid to guess."

"I had gooseberry fool."

"Wonderful," I said.

"No, really. It was delicious. If you haven't had gooseberries, you haven't lived." She yawned. "Why am I talking about food at this hour?"

"To keep my mind off Attilio," I said.

"I have better ways to do that," Jackie said.

"Just come," I said. "I may be rehearsing. Or in the slammer. But come anyway. I need you."

"Why would they put you in jail? You didn't do it, did you?"

"I don't think so," I said. "But there you are in London, and maybe your absence drove me to homicidal mania."

"You're silly." A long pause, then, "I love you."

"Me, too." I was too drained to say much more. "If you get to the airport and I'm not there—"

"You'll be with Miss Forest City."

"I'll ignore that. Come with your laurels."

"They'll probably stop me at Customs. Who would believe a suitcaseful of laurels?"

On that dizzy but reassuring note, we said good night.

"Alan, honey, pass me the jelly."

Sunlight was spilling through the tall windows of the dining room and spreading in pleasing patterns on the ornate marble floor. Arrayed on the breakfast table were bowls of peaches and apricots from the count's orchards, fresh-baked rolls from the count's ovens and your choice of chocolate, cappuccino or *caffè latte* to drink.

On this marvelous Veronese summer morning, it was my misfortune to have eyelids that needed propping open, a taste in my mouth like the last days of Pompeii and a budding headache that would undoubtedly require major brain surgery to cure. It was grossly unfair of Attilio to avenge himself this way on a total stranger.

"Sorry, no jelly," I mumbled. "Only marmalade."

Sabrina's face fell. "Damn, I wanted jelly. That mean old marmalade is so *bitter*. It just sticks in your mouth all morning long. Don't you think so, Alan?" Sabrina was in her usual morning rehearsal garb. Today's T-shirt was high-visibility orange. On the front it said MYRTLE BEACH DEPARTMENT OF PARKS & RECREATION. On the back it said LIFEGUARD. Neither the T-shirt nor Sabrina's shorts left much to the imagination, but my imagination was already overloaded. Maybe Khomeini was right about the *chador* after all.

"Sabrina, baby, you leave the boss man alone," Terry said. "He's brooding."

"That's right," I said. Sabrina was sitting with one long bare leg crossed over the other. I wondered vaguely how she'd managed to make the polish on her toenails almost match her T-shirt. Then I pulled myself together, more or less. "Let's see if we can grab a studio this morning. I'd like to go through our whole program."

"We can," Ralph said. "I've already booked it. We have room three from ten o'clock to noon."

"Good thinking," I said. Room three had a carved-stone fireplace and a wonderful set of frescoes of fauns chasing naiads. Even with a headache, I loved it. I got up from the table. "It's nine-thirty now. For once, let's start on time."

Amazingly, by ten-fifteen the Antiqua Players were in place and more or less tuned up.

"Let's take the whole thing from the top, okay? *El Marchese*, everybody! One, two, three, *one* . . ." Our opener was a short brisk dance that had come from a bawdy sixteenth-century street song. To make it as raucous as we could, I was playing a reed instrument called a shawm. The shawm is an ancestor of the oboe, and it sounds like a cross between a tenor saxophone and an irate duck. Once you get going on a shawm, you can make a lot of noise. By no stretch of the imagination can it be termed a scholarly noise. As a rule, that's fine. We want our audiences to know right away that we are musicians, not musicologists. But that morning, the sound did to my throbbing head what a jackhammer does to pavement. I was more than happy that we were following our hot-licks opener with a *padovano*, or pavane, a slow dance played on the nice quiet one-keyed wooden flute, lute and viola da gamba.

Fifteen minutes into the rehearsal and I'd forgotten all about Attilio and the count and his wine. I had a whole new set of problems to worry about.

"Terry?"

Terry raised his eyebrows, stuffed his krummhorn in his pocket and wandered over to where I was sitting.

"Listen," I said softly, so our rented cellist couldn't overhear. "I know Udo is a little wooden. But try to get this number off the ground."

"It's like playing with sand in your ears," Terry said. "The man is right on time but scratchy."

"Jackie will be back this afternoon."

"Yeah, good. But I wonder: is this kazoo"—he meant the krummhorn—"really right?"

"What would you use?"

"I don't know," Terry said, "but something's missing."

"No inner voices," Ralph said.

"Okay," I said. "What happens if David—"

"Not me," David said. "I can't make it punchy enough."

"Ralph, you play it."

Ralph sat back down at the harpsichord and fiddled with the stops. Stops govern which sets of strings sound when you touch the keys. Then he played the piece, which was a simple four-four dance tune with one or two odd twists in the melody. It sounded a lot more lilting than it did with Udo sawing away mechanically on the bottom line.

"One more time," Terry said. Ralph obliged, and Terry buzzed along on the krummhorn.

"It's better, but it still isn't right," I said. "Leave it, we'll get back to it later. Ralph, do you want to do your thing?"

"I *always* want to do my thing, you know that." When Ralph plays at rehearsal, all you have to do is turn pages for him, relax and listen. He's never unprepared. He always has his phrasings and fingerings worked out—his scores look like the hens have been running their Olympics on them—and his readings are getting more and more into the heart of the music.

The last Frescobaldi variation on the old tune *La Folia* is a deceptively easy exercise in two-part counterpoint. Ralph let each part have its say, and then he brought them together in a quiet close.

"That was so nice, Ralph, honey. I could just listen to you all day long," Sabrina said as she walked in the door. "Is it my turn now?"

David came forward with his theorbo. A theorbo is a bigger version of a lute, with more strings and longer strings and a deeper voice. David's been struggling with it for years. But it's a great accompanying instrument, and when we'd put Sabrina on the program to sing Monteverdi we'd decided that David's chance had come.

"Just a second," David mumbled, his head down over the tuning pegs. "Who was it who said that any lutenist who lives to be eighty has spent at least sixty years tuning up?" Ralph asked the air. "Probably some turkey, didn't know any harpsichordists," David said. "You all set, Udo?" Udo was standing in for Jackie, playing cello on the bass line. Udo wasn't really as bad as Terry said he was, he was just methodical. Now he gave a methodical nod. They both looked over at Sabrina. Sabrina was standing in place with her music in her hands, but her mind was far, far away.

I cleared my throat.

"Are you-all ready?" said Sabrina, suddenly returning to planet earth and her musical obligations.

"We-uns is ready," David said.

Quel Sguardo Sdegnosetto is one of Monteverdi's light, airy solo songs, all about disdainful glances and fiery darts that pierce the lover's breast. It opens with a mellow chord. Sabrina took a deep breath and I braced myself. But to my surprise, she didn't blast the first phrase out of the ball park. In fact, she made her way without explosion through the first twenty measures, remembered her one-bar rest and went blithely on. She really has a pretty chamber soprano, I found myself thinking. Maybe . . .

It was not to be.

"Measure twenty-nine," I said, sneaking a look at my English translation of the lyrics. "Sabrina, *'nembo di favile'* means 'cloud of sparks,' not smog over Los Angeles. You have to do the eighth-note run much lighter but *not* quicker. And *'favile'* doesn't rhyme with 'Billy.'"

"Again from halfway through twenty-seven, okay?"

Maybe it was the weather or something she'd eaten for breakfast or the feeling that she simply had to take a pop at me, but Sabrina decided to rebel. "Alan, I don't want to do it that way."

David, Ralph and Terry looked at me nervously. Udo looked at nothing at all.

The Antiqua Players are not a democracy.

I could feel my headache getting worse. "I don't give a good goddamn if you want to or not," I said. "You are bloody well going to start halfway through measure twenty-seven and sing that run exactly the way I tell you to sing it. And if I tell you to stand on your head and sing it, that's what you do, or else— Sabrina, for God's sake. Get her a Kleenex, someone."

The rebellion was over for the moment.

"I think you're a terrible person," she said, sniffing. "I'll do it your way, but it won't work."

"All right," I said, "from twenty-seven. I'll give you half a bar for free."

She counted back to measure twenty-seven, actually remembered to give David and Udo a cue, made the run as light as swansdown and sang like a lark all the way through to the end of the section.

I clapped enthusiastically. "That was terrific," I said. "How did you make *'favile'* come out right?"

Sabrina tried and failed to freeze me with disdain. "I just said 'five eel lay' to myself," she muttered.

Of such is the kingdom of music made.

We plowed through the rest of *Quel Sguardo*—actually, it wasn't too bad—and then through her other song, *La Violetta*, with yours truly playing violin to Terry's recorder on the instrumental repeats.

"You're not really a terrible person, Alan," Sabrina said when we could do no more, "just sometimes."

"You're not really a terrible singer, Sabrina," I began.

This time, Sabrina gave me her injured-artist stare. Her lower lip quivered. Slowly, she gathered up her music and walked toward the door. Halfway there, she turned and said with dignity: "I was trying to apologize, and all you want is just to hurt me." And out she went, swinging the massive door shut behind her.

I sighed.

"Lesson number one in music," Ralph said cheerfully. "Don't try to make jokes with singers."

Udo gave a guffaw. "This is I think a very complicated lady."

"Will anyone be offended," I said, "if we continue our rehearsal with the nonvocal material?"

"Alan, you have to remember that she's only a kid." Jackie and I were curled up together in a state of nature on the huge *letto matrimoniale* in our bedroom. All around us were the mementos of her London concert: newspapers folded open to the reviews, copies of the program, several publicity photos—"I love the one of you getting on the bus with your gamba," I said —and folios of music.

"Who are you calling a kid?" I held up a souvenir menu from the Ivy.

"Oh, that," Jackie said. "That's different. Sabrina really is a baby. This will be her first real appearance, and she's nervous."

"She may be a kid," I said, "and she may be nervous. But she is also vain, bitchy and a godalmighty pain in the ass. She is, in words of one syllable, a soprano."

"That's three syllables."

"When did you have the time to buy all of this stuff?" I asked, crumpling tissue paper.

On the bed were two new skirts and a dress from London, and she'd brought me back something very handsome indeed in cashmere.

"There's this place called Stover's, they have three shops and all the exchange students buy there. You can't believe how short the skirts are in London. And stop changing the subject."

"All right," I said. "If you'll clear off this bed so that we can put it to the purpose for which it was intended—"

Jackie giggled.

"—namely, sleep, I will promise to go tomorrow to Sabrina and apologize for being a heartless brute and chauvinist. That is, if Commissario Ratner doesn't get me first."

"*I* am going to get you first," Jackie said fiercely. She poured us each another half glass of white wine. "Drink this," she commanded, "and it will turn you into a swine. And then you can come after me, grunting and snuffling."

"And then can I get some sleep?"

"We'll see."

I drank.

"You know," I said between grunts and snuffles, "I like you better than acorns."

One must surmise that dancers have found
that the introduction of a few pleasing
variations lends grace . . .

Arbeau,
Orchesographie

CHAPTER SEVEN

With Jackie back among us and Udo out of the picture, rehears-als began to go more smoothly and we started to iron out our musical problems. Partly, it was because the viola da gamba blends better than the cello with preclassical instruments. But mostly, it was Jackie.

"You understand us," David said to her on her first day back.

"All I understand is that something's wrong at eighty-nine," Jackie said calmly. "Play it with me . . . There! Right there, you see?"

"You're getting louder so I'm getting louder," David said de-fensively.

"But I'm not getting louder."

"She's not," I said.

"She's not," Terry said.

"Okay, okay," said David, "Udo got louder, you're not getting louder. I can dig it. I'll play real soft, like this."

"Excellent," Terry said.

"Now see if you can get Alan to practice his fiddle parts," said Ralph.

"I thought you were my friend," I said.

"Alan French . . . ," Jackie said reproachfully.

I practiced: violin, flute, recorders, rebec, shawm, everything.

The work went on, mornings and afternoons for the next three days, until our timing glittered and our phrasings were right and we were a little sick of the music but not so sick of it that we were stale. Evenings, we went to Manny Gardi's *L'Ari-anna* section rehearsals and practiced with the singers.

There was only one interruption.

At breakfast on the second day—it was a Tuesday—Orlando the majordomo came to the table with a message. Commissario Ratner would be pleased if I would present myself at his offices to attest to my statement regarding the demise of Attilio Caspardino. When? "The commissario has sent a car for you, *signore.*"

I gulped down the last of my cappuccino. It wouldn't do to keep the cops waiting.

"If you're not back by noon," said Terry, "we'll call in the Marines."

I tried to guess what the police station would look like. Would it be a rusticated, fortresslike Veronese palazzo like the count's? Or, like the count's winery, something mundane but unexpected? In fact, after ten minutes of snaking through morning traffic, the police Alfa Romeo first paused at the gate, then pulled into the courtyard of one of those steel, glass and concrete confections that look as if clever schoolchildren put them together out of Lego parts.

I followed the driver through a sleek empty lobby and up a flight of stairs. The lighting in the corridors was indirect and discreet. The secretaries' desks were post-Bauhaus Good Design. No doubt there were cheery posters on the walls of the cells in the basement, and blankets in matching colors on the prisoners' cots.

Commissario Ratner rose politely as I entered his office. He looked different today. The nylon raincoat and the absurd hunting hat of Sunday were gone, of course, and in his neat dark suit and formal tie the commissario seemed much more the official of rank, much less the shabby cop. I sensed shrewdness as well as authority in his saturnine look.

"Please, Mr. French, be seated."

The Swedish modern armchair felt much less comfortable than it appeared.

"You are here, as you know, to fulfill the formality of acknowledging by signature the statement you made on Sunday. Here are copies, in English and Italian. If you wish, you may have a representative of your government present to advise you. But, speaking personally, I hope you will not insist." He gave his closed smile. "We are quite persuaded that you are in no way involved in this matter."

The typescripts looked thin and insubstantial. The commissario handed me one and gestured for me to read it through. It didn't take long. I hadn't had much to say.

When I was finished, he raised his eyebrows inquiringly.

"Fine," I said.

I signed my name half a dozen times, with one of Ratner's staff as witness. A secretary appeared to take away the papers. When she was gone, Ratner leaned back in his own chair and eyed me in his neutral fashion.

"Yes," he said, speaking a shade more intimately, "I am satisfied that you could have had nothing to do with this affair. And yet . . . His Excellency the count suggests that his cousin might have been involved with some"—he wrestled with the wording—"disreputed elements. That is to say, some gang. Frankly, I wonder."

He kept on looking at me while his left hand squeezed the fingers of his right hand as if to loosen the muscles. I noticed it because it's something I do myself when I'm warming up to practice. "Mr. French," he said, "I am going to take you into my confidence."

Oh, *no*, I thought. First the count, now the cop. Out loud, I said, "But . . . why?"

Now it was Ratner's right hand that was massaging the left.

"Attilio Caspardino was killed by a stab wound that entered his body on the left side below the . . . the . . ."

"Breastbone?" I volunteered. "Ribs?"

"Ribs, I thank you, and penetrated his heart. The wound was expertly given, and the weapon used was probably a thin sharp knife, sharp as to both the point and blade. The sanguination . . . the bleeding . . . was extensive. We have found matching blood traces, you understand, both in the vat where Caspardino was found and in another place a short distance away."

I was beginning to feel queasy. "Why are you telling me this?" I repeated.

Again Ratner ignored, or seemed to ignore, my question. "Our findings would argue an assassination, not a killing done in the heat of feeling as one would expect within a family."

"Family?" I said.

"Count Emilio Sabinetti is an important, respected personage in this region," said Ratner obliquely. "There is nothing, absolutely nothing, to connect him directly with the death of his cousin, who was . . . perhaps . . . less respected. Our researches have just begun. They will continue until we have a clearer portrait of Attilio Caspardino's activities and friendships.

"But even though it is evident that Caspardino's death came at the hands of a professional, and even if my superiors ridicule the idea"—Ratner grinned crookedly—"I cannot ignore my feeling that the count knows something or is in some way involved.

"I will naturally expect you to disagree with my . . . supposition. But nevertheless I ask for your assistance."

The last thing in this world I wanted was to get tangled up in a Veronese police investigation. But if there was one other thing in the world I didn't want, it was to get this very shrewd Veronese policeman mad at me.

"I'll help in any way that I can," I said dubiously, "but I don't see—"

"Mr. French, you will be busy with your playing for the *festivale*, Ratner said easily. "I know that. What I ask is simple. If you hear or see anything that sheds light on this affair, *even if it concerns Count Emilio Sabinetti or his associates*, telephone me, here or at my home.

"You will do this?"

I shrugged. "Do I have any choice?"

First, Ratner wrote his home number in small neat script on his business card. He handed the card to me. Then he said with a touch of acerbity: "No. You do not have any choice. A failure to cooperate with the police in a criminal investigation is itself a violation of our criminal statutes. For this, I could have you held pending a judicial inquiry. That would be . . . awkward. And of course disruptive of your performance schedule."

There was a hollow feeling in the pit of my stomach, exactly as Ratner intended there to be.

"No doubt my request makes you feel somewhat disloyal to the count," Ratner went on. "I appreciate your delicacy. But let me remind you that we are inquiring into a death by violence and that you owe a certain duty to the community and to us as its representatives. Let that suffice to ease your discomfort."

Score another one for the commissario.

After a few seconds of silence, Ratner nodded a dismissal. I got to my feet. But as I was leaving, he smiled almost pleasantly and said: "It is all right, Mr. French. We are not bloodless monsters, only bureaucrats. You may grow to love us. For myself, I look forward to your concert on Saturday."

All I could think of to say was, "I hope you enjoy it."

"*Arrivederlà*, Mr. French."

The same taciturn cop who had brought me drove me back to the Palazzo Sabinetti. Everybody was either practicing or at rehearsal. I was just in time to drink a quick cup of coffee, then grab my violin and hurry off to Manny Gardi's morning session. Manny's cold was better and he worked us hard on the instrumental segments of *L'Arianna*, the *sinfonietti* introducing the scenes and the *ritornelli* between vocal passages.

The notes weren't difficult—any competent string player could read his part at sight—but the openings and closes had to be on cue and the tone just right. After an hour on the podium, Gardi was sweating profusely and enjoying himself hugely, and we were beginning to give him the seamless sound and stopwatch timing he was asking us for.

I was having a good time, too, just playing and listening. For a while, I forgot all about the count, his cousin Attilio, the commissario and my new role as fink.

"Okay, all right already, *basta*, enough!" Manny threw down his baton, swore cheerfully, mopped his face with the pink bath towel he had brought with him for the purpose and dismissed us for the day.

Jackie and Ralph pushed their way toward me through the thicket of folding chairs, music stands and departing musicians.

"How did it go?" Ralph asked.

"Well, they haven't caught anybody yet, if that's what you mean," I said. "And they didn't use the rubber hoses on me. Not exactly, anyway."

"Are you okay?" Jackie asked anxiously.

"I'm fine," I said, but in fact I wasn't so fine. Now that the adrenaline had stopped flowing, the combination of the Ratner interview and the brisk rehearsal had left me feeling like Manny Gardi's damp bath towel.

"Come on," Ralph said decisively. "Let's get out of here and go someplace."

"And I know where," I said.

Across the Corso and down the block was the big *trattoria* that had become the official hangout for the festival's musicians and singers. They served fair pasta and drinkable coffee, and they were nice about letting people sit around. But that wasn't good enough for Ralph. So we walked past the Trattoria dell'Orso, turned down a narrow side street and ducked into an even narrower alley. Halfway down the alley was Wendy's.

This Wendy's bore no resemblance whatever to the burger joints of the same name in the good old U.S.A. A few lengths of shaky white picket fence propped up by metal supports defined an area of cobbles just big enough for four café tables. A faded green awning shaded the tables, but we never saw anybody sitting outside. At Wendy's, the customers ate inside, in a cramped square room with a big cooler at one end and Wendy at the other. It had taken Ralph and Terry nearly one whole day to find Wendy's and the better part of an evening for us to make friends with everybody in the place including Miele, the elegant toffee-colored restaurant cat. The service at Wendy's was languid. The food was sensational. Nobody from the festival except us ever came there.

Wendy, a thin ageless woman with a worried look, greeted us from behind the *cassa*.

"Un' orzata, figlia mia?" she said to Jackie. Jackie blushed to be called her daughter.

"Due, per piacere," I said.

Ralph ordered mineral water with lemon.

Wendy's niece brought the drinks and went back to do her schoolwork at the table nearest the kitchen.

I took a long sip of *orzata* and felt my blood-sugar level rise toward normal. For some reason also, the tepid, almond-flavored stuff is a great thirst quencher.

"Well. What *did* happen?" Ralph asked me.

"Nothing much. But it's a long way from over, and the commissario seems to think our friend and patron has something to do with it."

"The count?" Jackie's eyes were incredulous.

"He wasn't talking about Princess Di." I told them what there was to tell, including Ratner's "request" that I let him know anything I happened to find out.

"Nice," Ralph said dryly.

"What are you going to do?" Jackie asked.

"What *can* I do?" I said. "Obviously, I'm not going to go out of my way to squeal on the count. I'll keep out of his way as much as I can. But if he does say or do something—"

"I can't believe it," Jackie said. "Emilio *couldn't* have done it. Could he?"

"I guess it's possible," I said.

"Maybe it won't be a problem. Maybe nothing will happen," Ralph said. But he didn't say it very optimistically.

"Look," I said, "Ratner isn't going to leave it up to me. Whatever I do or don't do, he's going to come after me."

"Why?" asked Jackie.

"I think you're right," Ralph said to me. And to Jackie: "It's a way of putting pressure on the count."

"You mean when the Black Maria pulls up with three sinister policemen and screams are later heard from Alan's room, the count might decide to confess?"

"More or less," Ralph said.

"You know what?" said Jackie, "I think you should go talk to

the count and try to find out more about this Attilio. No, wait a
minute. I think *I* should go talk to the count."

Ralph laughed.

"Be serious," I said to Jackie. "We've got an opera opening in
three days and a recital the day after. You're not going to have
time to go interview the count, let alone make sense out of the
yarns he spins. It's bad enough that I'm involved. You stay out
of it."

"But Emilio would probably tell me things—"

"That's just it," I said. "You can make the mute stones speak.
And then along comes Ratner and we have to tell him what the
mute stones said, and then the count is really in trouble."

"Oh, well," Jackie said, "I guess you're right."

"To celebrate my escape from the *carabinieri* and your surren-
der," I said, "what about grabbing Terry and David and doing
that picnic we've been talking about?"

"And not rehearsing tonight?"

"And not rehearsing tonight."

"You are growing increasingly irresponsible, dear one,"
Ralph said. "I'll buy the wine."

CHAPTER EIGHT

Signora Wendy was only too happy to sell us our wine and pack
us a picnic supper as well. But her idea of sandwiches was slabs
of the local equivalent of Spam on buttered slices of American-
style white bread. She took some persuading to allow us to load
up on her provolone, her aunt's spicy homemade prosciutto
from the farm, black olives and torpedo-shaped loaves of *pane
fresco*. Fruit we would buy later, in the Piazza Erbe open-air
market.

Laden like donkeys, we made our way through the back
streets toward the Corso. We were about to round the last corner when Ralph stopped suddenly, ducked into the shadow of a
doorway and gestured for us to join him.

"What's going on?" I asked.

"Look," he said quietly. We looked where he pointed. "Isn't
that the count?"

Across the street was a small restaurant, smaller even than
Wendy's. The man at the table by the front window was indeed
the count. Dressed elegantly, as always, he was deep in conversation with someone whose face we couldn't quite see. The
count was leaning forward and speaking with intensity. Once or
twice, we saw him shake his head. Then, throwing some bills on
the table, he stood up: the movement was so abrupt that he
nearly knocked over his chair. He said a few more words to his
companion, who was still seated, then strode out of the restaurant. Before we could move, he had crossed the narrow street
and was heading straight for us. His face was pale and set. I

could even see the tiny pink flower he wore in his buttonhole. But without a glance or a word, he plunged by us and kept on going in the direction of the Corso.

I stared after the count with the others, until a movement at the entrance to the restaurant caught my eye. There, just coming out, was the other occupant of the count's table.

He seemed quite an ordinary figure, a smallish slender man in a light-colored suit, a plain tie and dark glasses. But something about his manner, so calm in contrast to the count's agitation, made me step deeper into the shelter of the doorway and pull Jackie and Ralph with me.

As he paused at the curb, a car slowed as if to pull up for him, but with a flick of his fingers he waved it on and it rolled quietly past him down the street. The man himself turned and began walking in the same direction. If he saw us, he gave no sign.

"What was that all about, I wonder?" I said as soon as the man had disappeared.

"I don't know," Ralph said, "but I really didn't like the look of that character, not one little bit."

"The two of you," Jackie said, "playing your little-boy games. I thought he looked perfectly respectable. Quite nice, in fact. And there you go diving into dark corners like a couple of muggers."

"Mugging him wouldn't be such a good idea," I said.

"If we're going on a picnic," Jackie said, "please let's get moving. I want to practice. And I want to wash my hair."

"For a picnic?" I asked.

"For you," said Jackie, taking my arm.

"Wow, tremendous!" Terry said. He put down an enormous sandwich of prosciutto, provolone and several less identifiable ingredients and took a long pull on the cold beer he'd made us stop to buy.

Our rented car was parked out of sight on a dirt track at the foot of the hill. We ourselves and our picnic had climbed the steep hillside and were ensconced on a narrow terrace just below the crest. Spread out before us was a fantastic view of other, lower hills, each terraced like our own and planted with olives. In some of the groves, grapevines had been trained up the trunks and lower branches of the trees. As a perfect touch, in the foreground a very small boy was coaxing four equally small goats down off a knob of rock into a farmyard. Beyond all of this was San Giorgio, and in the distance Verona itself.

Best of all, we were where we were by invitation. When we told them at the palazzo not to expect us for dinner because we were going on a picnic, Orlando the majordomo insisted on this place and no other. It was on his sister's farm, he said, which belonged to the count, and the count himself always came there during his summers in the country.

So there we sat in the midst of this feudal landscape, eating and drinking and wanting the long spring evening never to end.

I ate the last mouthful of my own gigantic sandwich, washed it down with Bardolino and thought dreamily of how wonderful it would be to live forever on a hill farm in the Veneto.

"We could grow grapes and olives and bask in the sun and give recitals in the church on Sundays," I murmured to Jackie. "Like Casals at Prades."

"Mmmm. Are there any more plums, Pablo darling?"

"You've already had six."

"I know, but they're so good." Jackie sat up and reached for the bag of fruit.

"Hey, Jackie, you got sunburnt," David said. "On your nose."

"Is it really red?"

"I think you look adorable," I said.

"Yes, but I was going to wear my white dress for the concert. If my nose is too red, I can't wear white."

"Relax," I said. "This is Tuesday and our concert isn't until Saturday. Besides, your nose isn't that red."

"It's pretty red." Jackie had fished a compact out of her big canvas carryall and was making faces at herself in the mirror.

"It will probably peel," David said lugubriously.

"Thanks," said Jackie.

"Have some more wine," Ralph said gravely, filling her paper cup. "It will help you forget."

We all had more wine, except Terry. He had more beer.

"I don't ever want to go back to Verona," David said.

I looked at my watch. "My God, it's nearly eight o'clock."

"Who cares?" David and Terry chorused.

Nobody cared, including me. It was nearly nine o'clock, with the mosquitoes working up a Saturday-night thirst in the failing twilight, before we could bring ourselves to pack up our leftovers and make our way down to the car.

By the time we dropped off the car at the rental agency and walked back down the Corso, it was closer to ten. David, Ralph and Jackie decided to go join the mob at the Trattoria dell'Orso, but the events of the day had caught up with me and I was ready for bed.

"I'm tired, too," Terry announced, so together we sauntered to the palazzo. I wanted to thank Orlando for his kindness, but he had gone home for the day and his little booth was empty.

We were just crossing the courtyard when the whisper came from the dimness by the silent fountain.

"Mr. French . . ."

"It's the count," I said softly. "It must be."

"Okay," said Terry, "whoever he is, let's check him out."

Count Emilio was seated on the coping of the fountain. He was wearing the same suit he had been wearing when we'd seen him earlier. The little pink flower in his buttonhole was dry and faded. When he stood up to meet us, his movements were stiff with fatigue.

"I must talk with you," he said. "In private."

"What you say to me, you say to Mr. Monza."

The count bowed ever so slightly to Terry. "Very well, if you think it is necessary. Let us go to my office. We can be quiet there."

He led us through unlit public rooms and high-ceilinged hallways to the farthest wing of the palazzo. I expected the massive oaken tables and carved chests, tall candelabra and ancestor portraits of tradition, but instead the count's private quarters were light and airy and filled with elegant contemporary furnishings and vivid modern paintings.

His inner office itself was more like a rich intellectual's hideaway than like a place where business is done. Two walls were lined with bookshelves, and some of the books on them looked well handled. A single Cubist still-life adorned a third wall.

"Braque?"

The count looked pleased. "No. Everyone thinks so, but it is by Gris." As he remembered why we were there, his pleasure vanished. "Sit down, gentlemen. I will not offer you a drink now. Later, perhaps . . ."

We took seats and waited.

"I have told you about Attilio," said the count at last.

"You have told me a great many things," I said. "Some of them were even true."

He winced. "I am sorry. Foolishly, I thought it was . . . not necessary . . . to tell you the whole of the story. I am sorry.

"Now, if you will listen, I will tell you everything. Because I need your help."

I glanced at Terry. He shrugged and nodded. "We'll listen," I said.

Count Emilio hunched deeper in his armchair. "The other night, I told you that I was in debt to the bankers. Also, that I had sold my wine for a good price to some *negozianti*, some wine merchants, in Marseille, even though prices this year were very low."

"I remember," I said.

"But this I did not tell you, that I had in mind to take advantage of the poor market."

"How?" Terry asked, looking interested.

"I sold my wine a second time."

It was my turn to ask how.

"When you sell new wine," the count explained, "you sell it before you make it. Sometimes even before the grapes are harvested. Your buyer pays you some money in hand, the rest when the wine is made and shipped.

"The day I received the offer from the merchants of Marseille, I also received an offer from an importer in America. In Jersey City."

"Oh-oh," said Terry.

"I saw a way of quickly making some extra money. Of getting ahead of my debts. So I said yes to the second offer as well as to the first.

"I have a neighbor, a big grower. His vineyards are as good as mine. Well, maybe not so well tended. But his wine is excellent and he too needed money. I knew he had wine to sell."

"So you went short," Terry said.

"*Scusi?*"

"You sold wine you didn't have at a high price, hoping you could cover yourself at a lower price before shipping time."

"Yes," said the count. "Only—"

"Only what?" asked Terry.

"My neighbor found out. All my neighbors. I would have paid them more than the *negozianti* were offering, although naturally less than I myself was receiving. But they wouldn't sell. Not one liter. I raised my price, but they still waited. *They wouldn't sell.*

"It was Attilio!" The count's voice suddenly went hoarse and he banged a fist gently on his desk top. "Attilio found out what my needs were. He told them to wait. He betrayed me!"

Terry and I exchanged glances.

The count saw us. "I know what you are thinking," he said quickly. "You are thinking, this is a reason for . . . avenging myself . . . upon Attilio. But in truth I did not know this before Attilio was killed. I worked it out afterward. I now think that Attilio wanted to meet with me that night in Sant'Ambrogio to tell me what he had done and to threaten to do more, unless—"

"Unless you paid him off?" Terry asked.

"Exactly."

"Keep it all in the family, right?" said Terry. "Nice guy."

"Then you believe me?"

Terry looked at me and shrugged. "We want to believe you," he said, "and what you're saying *could* be okay. Let's say we don't not believe you, for now, anyway. Somebody else could have done it. Right, Alan?"

"That's about it," I said.

"But that's not really all there is to it," Terry said to the count, "whether we believe you or not. I mean, even if you didn't lay a glove on cousin Attilio, you still have a problem, right?"

"You are right, my friend," said the count.

"Like, where are you going to get more wine?"

"Of course."

"Well, hell," Terry said. "There must be plenty of wine around."

"Of course," the count said again. "But those who have it do not wish to sell it at my price."

"You'll have to up the price some," Terry said.

"I cannot," said the count. "If I raise it again, I will not have enough cash to cover the payments."

"Can't you borrow the extra cash?" I asked.

The count smiled wryly. "If I could borrow, I would not be speculating."

"True," I said.

We all fell silent.

After a couple of moments, Terry said: "You really are between the rock and the hard place. When is post time?"

"*Scusi?*"

"Sorry," Terry said. "I mean, when do you have to deliver the wine?"

"In exactly seventeen days from today, at the winery. Both parties, of course, will be expecting full delivery."

Terry whistled.

"Let me see if I've got this straight," I said. "You have enough money from the first sale to cover the cost of the wine you need for the second sale—if you can get the second batch or armload or whatever at a reasonable price. If not, you will be in trouble."

"I will be destroyed," the count said. "To disappoint the buyers from Marseille I know would be dangerous. To disappoint the buyers from New Jersey could be worse than dangerous. To disappoint them both would be to commit suicide. Only today, the representative of the Marseille syndicate lectured me on the need to meet my contract. The others will no doubt be in Verona shortly."

"One thing for sure," Terry said. "You need more wine."

"Indeed," said the count.

"Just out of curiosity," I said, "how much more wine do you need?"

"One million liters, and I can pay no more than fourteen hundred lire per liter plus shipping."

Again Terry whistled. "That's about eighty cents. So the whole deal will cost you about eight hundred thousand dollars?"

"Correct."

"You must be about tripling your money, then?" Terry asked carelessly.

The count made no reply.

"Okay, okay," Terry said, "I won't ask. But that's a lot of lettuce. Money, I mean."

"Yes," said the count. "A great deal."

"You said you wanted our help," I said. "What do you have in mind this time? Not money, I hope?"

"No, of course not money," said the count. "Orlando told me that Commissario Ratner sent for you this morning. I do not know what passed between you—"

"I wouldn't be surprised if someone had told you that, too," I said.

"Unfortunately, no. But I surmise that the commissario has asked you to . . . tell him things that you hear. He may even threaten you if you do not tell him.

"I do not know how to adjust my business difficulties. But I certainly must have a week, two weeks—enough time to breathe. Otherwise . . ." The count made a gesture of helplessness. "I beg you. I beg you not to tell the commissario of my problems with the wine."

"He's a cop," Terry said. "Cops always find out things like that."

"I agree," said the count. "But it will be at least two weeks before he learns. In that two weeks, perhaps, I can find some answer. Afterward, if I cannot, who knows if I will still be alive?"

I stared at the count, wondering tiredly if he really believed that his friendly customers would take nondelivery so seriously. Wondering also if this story wasn't a piece of fiction, an improvisation out of Lampedusa or Moravia. Then I thought about the man we'd seen in front of the restaurant that afternoon, the small man who seemed so nondescript and yet somehow so frightening.

"All right," I said. "I will keep quiet about the wine. For now. But if at the end of the festival nothing is resolved—that's two weeks from tomorrow—I will go to Commissario Ratner. That okay with you, Terry?"

Terry nodded. For some reason, he was looking pleased with my answer. "I was going to suggest the same thing."

"Gentlemen—" the count began.

"Don't thank us, Count," I said. "I hope you can work it out, that's all." Suddenly and uncontrollably, I yawned.

"Yeah, I'm tired, too," said Terry. "Count, you'll have to excuse the two of us. It's been a long day."

With further protestations of gratitude, the count showed us back to our quarters. Terry said good night and bounced blithely past me up the stairs. Jackie was peacefully asleep when I tiptoed into the room. Five minutes later, I joined her in slumberland.

What is done once must not be immediately repeated a second time.

Cornazano,
Art of Dancing

CHAPTER NINE

At breakfast, I bit into a hard roll and shuddered: for one terrible second I thought I'd lost a filling. It turned out to be a false alarm, but it was no way to begin the day.

Jackie, farm girl that she was, was pitching into a major breakfast. Berries, they looked like raspberries, eggs . . .

"Where'd you get bacon and eggs?" I demanded.

She looked smug. "Unlike you, I am not surly and unmannerly to the people in the kitchen in the morning, probably because I get a good night's sleep every night, and so they oblige me."

"Every night?"

"Most nights. Which reminds me—"

"Where was I last night until late?" I said.

"Yes, where were you?"

"I was in a small, intimate bistro—"

"This is Verona, silly, not Paris—"

"Drinking cognac, no, all right, grappa—"

"With a beautiful *Fräulein.*"

"How did you guess?"

"Terry squealed on you. He told me everything."

So much for male bonding.

Just then, Terry himself made an entrance through the double doors at the end of the dining room. Like me, he looked tired. But unlike me, he was freshly shaven, fragrant with aftershave and abrim with energy. "Hey, Alan. Guess what?"

"You've lost your *L'Arianna* music again."

"Naw. Nothing to do with music."

"Tell *me*, Terry," Jackie said. "Our chief is in a mood."

He jerked his head in Jackie's direction. "She know any-thing?"

"Usually," I said.

"What's that mean?" Terry said.

"She doesn't know yet, but she will soon."

"Would you like me to leave?" Jackie asked, too politely.

"No," I said. "But to clue you in, I have to go back to our previous conversation and tell you where I was—where Terry and I were—last night."

"You were with the count," Jackie said.

"How do you know that?" I said.

"You told me. Last night. Just before you fell asleep."

"Oh. Well, we were with the count and he told us another version of his troubles. This one I think may be true. At least, it's a lot truer than the others."

"Right," Terry said. "You know what the guy does, Jackie? He goes short his entire wine crop to a second buyer. And the worst thing, can you believe, he does it to a guy from New Jersey."

"He goes short? Terry . . . Alan, do *you* know what he's talk-ing about?"

Between us, Terry and I managed to explain what the count had done, or said he'd done.

"Now I understand," Jackie said. "He's sold something he hasn't got in the hope he can go out and get it before it's too late and make some money after all."

"Close enough," I said.

"His big problem," Terry said, "is, he hasn't got enough wine to cover himself and nobody will sell it to him. I just solved his problem."

"That's it," I said. "He's got two buyers and— Terry, what did you just say?"

"I solved his problem," Terry repeated, grinning. "I got him some wine."

Jackie pushed back her chair. "I think I *will* leave."

"You stay right here," I said, grabbing her arm. "I want a witness. Now, Terry, give us a break. Take this a step at a time. What do you mean, you got the count some wine?"

"My uncle," Terry said, still grinning.

"Oh, Christ," I said, and Jackie said "Christus," which adds up to a double exclamation of distress.

Terry's uncle. Monza's in Queens. Monza's, with orange and aqua lights and walnut trim and a parking lot big enough to accommodate a fair-sized Shea Stadium crowd. Monza's must sell *oceans* of Italian wine.

"No wonder you seemed so interested last night," I said. "I should have paid more attention . . . but I was tired. Okay. So what did you do?"

"What do you think? I went upstairs, went in the booth and got on the horn to Queens. My uncle was there, the bar, watching them set up for dinner. I told him, he said, Sure, no problem, gave me two numbers. One in Bardolino, right near here, okay? But the other one, if the count wants good stuff really cheap, that's the one to call."

"Where's that one?"

"Yugoslavia."

"*Yugoslavia?*"

"Yeah, what's so terrible about that?"

Jackie and I eyed each other helplessly. I think we both sensed what was coming. "Nothing, I guess," I said.

"There you go," Terry said airily. "My uncle says, we play it right, we ought to clear easily eighty, ninety thousand on the deal."

"Now, *wait* a minute," I said, exactly like Jack Benny on the old radio shows.

"What deal?" Jackie chimed in. "And make it quick," she added. "We're supposed to be rehearsing in ten minutes."

Terry held up a hand. "No big thing," he said. "It can wait. In fact, I'd just as soon wait until Ralph and David can hear. Meanwhile, I'll get myself some breakfast."

Jackie and I swallowed our impatience while Terry swallowed six or seven rolls smeared with peach jam, a generous cut of salty ham and two huge glasses of milk.

"I don't see how you can *talk* after that," Jackie said as we left the dining room to collect our instruments, "let alone play."

"Practice," Terry said as he sprinted up the stairs.

It didn't take us long to fill in Ralph and David on what had been happening. Then Terry jumped in to explain his deal. "All we have to do is call up these vintners in Bled—"

"Where's that?" Ralph asked.

"Who cares?" said Terry. "Some burb in Yugoslavia. All we have to do is make a phone call, mention my uncle's name—he says the one brother speaks good English—tell them we want to make a big buy. We say how much, get a price and wire them the okay. They confirm, we send them the down payment and they ship. When we get the goods, we send them the rest of the dough. Simple."

"Where do *we* get the dough?" David asked in his languid fashion, as if the whole matter were too remote to be worth thinking about.

"The count," Terry answered. "You got to remember, he's desperate. He doesn't come up with some wine, that little guy we told you about is going to do something very bad. If we can show him the wine, believe me, he'll put up the cash."

"Sounds wild to me," Ralph said.

If *Ralph* thought something was wild, a Mississippi riverboat gambler would have gone fifty miles out of his way to avoid it.

But Terry paid no attention. "How can we lose?" he asked rhetorically. "No way. My uncle says we can buy the wine for seventy cents a liter. We sell it to the count for eighty cents. Bam! We make a hundred grand."

Silence ensued, as each member of the Antiqua Players contemplated what his or her share of a hundred thousand dollars might mean. But all too soon, the happy spell was broken.

Oddly enough, it was David, our supposedly unworldly David, who brought us back to reality. "How does the count get the wine?" he asked.

Terry looked at him pityingly. "They ship it to him," he explained. "First it goes in trucks. Then they put it on a boat—"

"Won't they be mad?" David asked vaguely.

"Won't *who* be mad?" said Terry, mystified.

"The buyers. They think they're getting the count's own

wine, don't they? They're watching him. How is he going to sneak this other wine into his garage or wherever you keep wine? And even if he does it, what if it's not as good? They shoot the count, right? I mean, that's what I'd do if I were them, and I wouldn't pay the bill if I were them, so what happens to the money?"

Terry didn't utter a word. But a flush darkened his olive skin. Nobody else said anything, either.

It was sad to say goodbye to our hundred thousand dollars.

I was about to break the silence with some brilliant bit of consolation like Easy come, easy go, when David cleared his throat. "What we need," he said, "is samples."

"Samples," Terry repeated softly. Slowly, his flush subsided. "You're right, you dumb lute-picking bastard." A broad grin illuminated his face. He reached over and affectionately ruffled David's hair. "We need samples. We need guarantees. Somebody's gonna have to stay with that wine from the time it's put on the train to the time it gets to the count's warehouse."

"Terry," Jackie said warningly, but it was too late. Hope had begun to dawn again.

"We can do it!" Terry exclaimed. "Please, guys." He turned to me. "Don't you want twenty big ones? Don't you?"

"Sure," I said, "who doesn't?"

"Then help me figure this out."

"I'll help anybody do anything," I said. "*After* rehearsal."

"You've got to be kidding," Terry said.

"Not me," I said. "May I remind you that we've got a concert on Saturday and another one the following Wednesday, and all the wine deals in the world won't help us if we screw up now. So let's ice the wine for a while, Terry, what do you say?"

"Hear, hear," Ralph said, pulling up a rickety chair to the harpsichord.

Jackie was already tuning up to Ralph's A.

Terry shook his head. "I don't *believe* this," he muttered. "You'd rather do music than get rich." But he spread open his music and picked up his tenor recorder anyway.

As I hoped it would, work took our minds off the count's

dilemma and Terry's get-rich-quick solution. We worked hard, too. I made Ralph and Terry go over their little *ballo* seven times, with Ralph forsaking the keyboard for the sackbut or trombone and Terry supplying a jazzy accompaniment on drum.

I even sweet-talked Sabrina into rehearsing *La Violetta.*

"Please, Alan, honey," she said when I cornered her in the lounge, "I have to save myself for tomorrow."

Tomorrow was the dress rehearsal of *L'Arianna*, and critics would be about the place. All the singers were lurking around as nervous as cats.

"Just one take," I pleaded. "I'm switching from violin to treble viol, and I want to get the part right or we're going to sound awful."

"You promise you won't get mad and yell at me like you did the last time?"

I promised. I even promised her my violet Arcangelo Corelli sweatshirt if she'd do the number.

"Okay. One time."

Sabrina didn't strain herself, but at least she didn't keep coming in half a bar early. As soon as she was finished, I thanked her profusely and shooed her out of the room.

"Okay," I said to the others, "let's knock it off."

"You mean I can talk?" said Terry.

"You can talk," I said.

He did talk, and the rest of us joined in, and in the end we had a sort of plan.

I was to go to the count—"He's your *goomba*, "Terry said; "for some weird reason, he trusts you"—and sound him out about buying wine. If the count seemed interested, I should find out what kind of wine he wanted, and how much. We would then get him samples and prices and line up shipping.

"After that," Terry said, "we'll see."

" 'Oh, what a tangled web we weave,' " Ralph quoted oracularly.

"What's that supposed to mean?" I demanded.

"What do you tell Commissario What's-his-name when he shows up?"

"Ratner." How could I have forgotten about Ratner? "I don't know what to tell him."

"You better think of something, great leader," Ralph said. "He hasn't forgotten you, I'm sure."

"Tell him part of the truth," said Jackie. "Tell him the count feels Attilio was up to something shady and is upset about it, but you don't know what it was."

"Don't get put in jail," David said.

"Don't what?" I said, startled.

"Not until you get the count to make the wine buy."

"David," I said, "I'll do my very best."

"I'll make sure you do," Jackie said.

"What are you talking about?" I said.

"I'm coming with you."

The corridors and public rooms of the count's quarters, silent and empty the night before, were livelier by day. Men in sober business suits were coming and going, and in one antechamber Jackie and I saw a whole family, husband, wife and four children, clustered together nervously on a wooden bench beneath an immense painting in a gilt frame.

"They've probably come to complain about the lease," I whispered kiddingly, but in the next breath I realized that it could perfectly well be true. To us, Count Emilio Sabinetti was a pleasant fellow with trouble on his hands. But to his own people, the count would be a powerful presence, a dispenser of jobs and money and housing and protection. A godfather. And clearly, nobody to trifle with.

I glanced uneasily at Jackie, but it was too late to turn back. The gorgon at the reception desk in the count's outer office was eyeing us balefully.

"*Sì?*"

I told her that we wished to see Count Emilio.

"You have an appointment?" the gorgon asked. I could almost hear the hissing of the snakes that wreathed her brow.

No, I admitted, we had no appointment.

"Well, then," she said, lifting one skinny black-clad shoulder in a contemptuous shrug.

Just then, thank God, the door of the inner office opened and the count himself looked out and saw us.

"Mr. French! And Miss Craine! What a delightful surprise! Come in, come in!"

Ignoring the gorgon, who seemed to be saying that we were upstarts who had destroyed the whole day's schedule, the count waved us inside and shut the door firmly.

"*Dio!*" he said, "that one! I keep her there for protection, and she is loyal and efficient, I grant you. But as beautiful as you, Miss Craine, she is not. But now, how may I help you? Is everything all right with the music?"

I assured him that there were no problems with the music. In fact, I said, instead of raising a problem we had come in the hope of helping him solve one.

The count raised his eyebrows.

"It has to do with wine," I said.

"With wine?"

"With your difficulty in securing it."

The eyebrows remained up. "Mr. French, I had no idea that you were an expert in the wine industry."

"I'm not," I said. "Far from it. But Mr. Monza, who was with me last night, is knowledgeable."

"You amaze me," said the count. Then, sharply, he asked: "Why are you coming to me like this?"

"For two reasons," I told him. "One: I am tangled up in your difficulties. My friends and I think that helping you will help us. Two: as a straightforward commercial transaction in which we, as middlemen, can earn some money."

"I thought money might enter into it," the count said. "Continue."

Rapidly, I filled in the picture. I explained that we thought we had located a supplier willing to part with ample quantities of wine at reasonable prices and ready to ship promptly.

"What, in your expert opinion, are reasonable prices?" the count asked, his voice politely ironic.

"Seventy cents a liter in bulk, plus shipping," I replied, as instructed.

"For wine of what quality?"

"That I frankly do not know," I told him. "But we would assume the responsibility of providing samples in advance."

"Hmm. You would certainly have to do that, I agree. Now, might one know the identity of your supplier?"

I shook my head.

The count's smile showed his teeth. "I thought that might be the case. Well, Mr. French, Miss Craine, I am sorry. I appreciate your efforts on my behalf, but I do not care to buy any wine at this time."

Damn.

"If that's your decision, then of course there's nothing more to say," I said. "I'm sorry to have disturbed you. Jackie, don't you think we've taken up enough of the count's time?"

"We have," said Jackie, "but Alan told me about your wonderful Juan Gris and he was right, it *is* wonderful. Thank you for letting me see it."

"Thank you for coming," the count said to her. "It is always a pleasure to see you again." Perhaps I was mistaken, but I thought I detected a slight but significant emphasis on that last "you." Oh well, friendship is fleeting.

We were almost out the door when the count suddenly called to me. "Mr. French!"

I turned.

"Tell me the truth. How quickly could your supplier furnish samples?"

We were back in the ball game.

But being back in the game doesn't necessarily mean winning.

By the time we left his office, fifteen minutes later, the count had handed us a typed sheet on which were the specifications of the wine he wanted. These were almost as detailed, I was surprised to discover, as engineering specifications. The count wanted a dry white varietal table wine; grape type, Sauvignon

Blanc (No. 1) or Welschriesling (No. 2); grade, premium *only;* region, not specified; alcohol content, 12 percent; quantity, no less than 500,000 liters of each variety; availability, immediate; price (maximum), eighty-one and a half cents per liter.

With the spec sheet went a preliminary agreement to cover the expense of providing sample bottles of the wines.

We thanked the count and took our leave. We were eager to get back to the others and put Terry to work on the phone, and I was about to say something boastful to Jackie when she grabbed my arm and the words froze in my throat.

Seated in a corner of the count's antechamber was the small man in gray we had seen in the count's company the day before.

I stared at him for several seconds. There was really nothing exceptional about his appearance. His gray suit was made of some smooth fabric like sharkskin. A white handkerchief peeked out of the breast pocket. His black shoes gleamed with polish. I saw no deliberately loose tailoring, no telltale bulge in an armpit, no sign at all of weaponry. If anything, the man's face looked refined, pleasantly scholarly. But this man was no sort of scholar.

As soon as we started across the room, he glanced up, saw us and came swiftly over to stand directly in front of us, blocking our path.

"*Scusi* . . . excuse me," I murmured, moving to one side to avoid him. But he moved, too, still barring our way. Short of pushing him aside, there was nothing I could do.

The gorgon guarding the count's office rose suddenly, seized her handbag and left the room, her heels clacking in hasty rhythm on the stone floor.

"Mr. Alan French." The man's voice was slightly hoarse, his English accented but fluent.

I nodded.

"And Mrs. French?"

"Miss Craine."

"I have seen you one or two times with Count Emilio."

"Yes," I said, "we are—"

He overrode my answer without raising his own voice, the way some deaf people do.

"You understand, the count has had a recent tragedy in his family."

That was one way of looking at it, I suppose.

"At such a time, people should be left alone. So . . . I beg you to leave him alone. Entirely alone." He punctuated these words with a formal little nod, but he was not being civil. He was issuing an order.

"Just a second," I said. "Who are you?"

"You should not be so curious," he said reprovingly. "It is not mannerly. But if you do not know, Commissario Ratner will perhaps tell you."

He stood aside then, and let us pass, but I felt his gaze on the back of my neck as we made our way to the door.

"You know," I said to Jackie, "I don't think that dude likes me." What I really meant, of course, was that this was as unfriendly a character as I had ever met, and that I wanted no part of him whatever.

"I wonder if we should be going on with this," Jackie said in a small voice.

"What? Oh, sure, it'll be okay. He just wants what the count wants, to keep us from talking to the cops." Big Daddy Alan, radiating confidence and good cheer.

"You're scared, too," Jackie said promptly.

"You're right," I said, "but I'm also greedy. And you know what that means."

"I do know. How do you say 'parole board' in Yugoslavian?"

Bacchus, that great leader called Dionysus,
taught his soldiers . . . dancing and military marches
to the sound of the drum.

Arbeau,
Orchesographie

CHAPTER TEN

Wine. The sugary juice of the grape, fermented, transformed
into an intoxicant by cunning little yeasts, allowed to age and
change in casks, then taken to market in clay vessels, stone
crocks, glass bottles and even leather bags. And because it set-
tleth the stomach and maketh glad the heart, man has drunk the
stuff since time out of mind, attributing its virtues to the gods.

Right now, I thought, a little help from the gods would be
more than welcome. "Terry. Terry?"

He made a face at me from inside the phone booth. Then he
slid open the door and, still with the receiver to his ear,
shrugged awkwardly. "They're having a little trouble getting
through."

"Funny," I said, "I thought Bled was a world crossroads of
telecommunications."

"Take it easy. They're working on it."

Suddenly, he grimaced and shut the door of the booth. I could
see him through the glass, talking animatedly into the mouth-
piece and gesticulating with his free hand. Then he nodded vio-
lently twice or three times and abruptly hung up.

"Well?" I demanded.

"They got through to the winery. They're trying to locate the
salesman, but he's out somewhere. They'll call back."

"They'll call back! We're due to leave in"—I looked at my
watch—"seventeen seconds."

From where I was standing, I could see musicians lugging
their instruments downstairs, on their way to the bus. It was
dress-rehearsal day for *L'Arianna* and we were being driven

across town for our first crack at playing in San Zeno. Ralph and Jackie had already gone over in a van with the harpsichord, Ralph to watch over the move and Jackie to watch over Ralph, who tends to become emotional whenever anybody else handles the instrument he's playing.

Now the singers were trooping down the stairs. I caught a glimpse of Sabrina, smiling happily amid a group of burly males. Maybe those hours of coaching would pay off.

I checked to see that my violin and flute were still where I'd put them. They were, along with Terry's instruments, our folding music stands and both plump folders of music.

I was almost ready to abandon Terry and his scheme and dash for the bus when the phone gave its gurgling ring.

Again Terry shut the door, and again he began a vigorous conversation. This time, however, he soon stopped talking. A broad smile spread over his face as he listened, and he winked at me through the glass and waggled his circled thumb and forefinger triumphantly.

At last, he hung up and emerged from the booth.

I didn't let him utter a word until we were safely on the bus and crossing the Adige near the Arsenale. Then, under cover of the chatter around us, I asked him what had happened.

"It went good," he said. "They're ready to do business."

He would have said more, but just then one of Sabrina's fellow artists, a tenor sitting three seats away, let loose with some lusty vocalization, and normal speech became impossible. And as he finished, so did our bus ride. The bus swung left and recrossed the river, then squeezed into a narrow *viale* and pulled to a stop at a side entrance to San Zeno.

"They got our specifications and they're sending someone here with samples," Terry said *sotto voce* as we followed the others into the vast church.

"They work fast," I muttered back. "When?"

"What would you say to tomorrow?"

"Fantastic!" I said, and meant it. Then we had to separate, Terry to warm up, I to sneak up behind Jackie and breathe in her ear.

"Monster," she said unconcernedly.

"You spotted me coming in."

"Yes, you were late as usual. Otherwise—"

"Otherwise you never would have bothered to watch," I said.

"That's almost true."

"I *think* we're getting the wine," I said.

"Sit down, Alan. Manny's looking at us. Is that why you're so late?"

"Tell you later," I said, unfolding my stand and settling myself behind it to tune. "An A, Ralph, please."

"All right, now, everybody," Manny Gardi said from the podium. "We want to run through the entire first act if we can, with no breaks, for timing and to get used to these acoustics." As he spoke, his voice reverberated through the length and breadth of the huge basilica.

We laughed.

"There you are. We'll sound awfully echoish at first," he went on, "but you have to remember that in performance there will be a whole audience full of nice suits and dresses to absorb the sound. So take it easy, especially you strings, but not *too* easy.

"Okay? Let's go!"

And away we went, into the opening measures of the overture.

"Oh, Christ!" Manny groaned loudly. "Stop!"

We ground to a halt.

In all, there were about twenty players, five of us and fifteen others. The others included a spare flautist, a pair of oboists, eight violinists and violists (not including me), Udo and one other cellist, a string bass player and a percussionist. By New York Philharmonic standards, we were a tiny ensemble, but in the nave of San Zeno, we made one hell of a racket.

Manny Gardi looked exasperated. He didn't use a baton, so he rapped on his music desk with a pencil to get our attention. The resonance in the nave was so strong that the tiny noise sounded like a pistol shot. "We're going to have to lighten this up a lot," he said.

In the next ten minutes, while we waited, Manny rescored the entire overture.

As he scribbled away, sweating even in the cool church and mopping his face with his towel, he talked, telling us what he was doing and why, giving us his changes and sometimes asking us how we thought a particular passage should be orchestrated. It was a lesson in musical craftsmanship at the hands of a first-rate practitioner. Even though I had my doubts about the outcome, I was impressed.

"All right," Manny said at last, "let's try it."

The first violinist put down her London *Times* crossword and took up her instrument. Ralph, who had been helping her, wriggled around on his bench to face the keyboard. Everybody else stopped whatever he was doing. Those of us who had survived Manny's cuts made ready to play.

". . . and three and four and *go!*"

Obediently, we went. It was better, but it wasn't right.

"Okay . . . hold it!" Manny's face tightened with frustration. "Now what the hell do I do?" I heard him say under his breath as he stamped around on the podium and glared at the music. It was obvious that he had to do something: the music was so blurred that a listener couldn't follow it.

Manny had stepped down from the podium to confer with a worried-looking man in a dark suit, probably the official in charge of San Zeno.

"Better split us up," a voice behind me said.

In the middle of his conversation, Manny stopped short. "Better do what? Who said that?"

"I did." It was David, looking soulful and hugging his theorbo.

Manny slapped his forehead. "Of course! What an idiot I am! Why didn't I think of that?"

Locating groups of instrumentalists at strategic intervals for dramatic and acoustic effect was something Renaissance music masters did all the time, especially in churches. It took Manny Gardi about five self-reproachful minutes to reorganize us into two smaller ensembles, place one by a pillar halfway down the nave and the other much closer to the stage, which was right in front of the wide staircase leading to the crypt. Then he spent another five rescoring the overture once more so that first one group played, then the other.

"Can everybody see me?" he called from the podium. Everybody could. "All right . . . from the top."

With fewer people playing at any one time, the texture of the music lightened and the blurriness disappeared. I thought we sounded fine, but Manny is a perfectionist. He stopped us after a dozen bars.

"Much better, absolutely. But you strings, I want your attack much smoother, much less grunt, okay? From measure ten . . . three and four and . . . yes. *Yes!* Go on, go on . . ."

Manny was so delighted by the end of the overture that he almost had to be forcibly restrained from making us repeat it. But reason prevailed and we went right on into the opening act one choral number. Or rather, we would have gone on, except that the chorus, supposed to be present in attractive stylized nymph-and-shepherd costume, was, first of all, not present but outside on a bus and, second of all, not in nymph-and-shepherd costume but in the picaresque mixture of jeans, T-shirts, striped open-necked sports shirts, tank tops, leather vests, sandals, running shoes, high-laced boots and sunglasses that you find on all choruses in all countries everywhere.

Manny moved around restlessly while this scruffy crew assembled itself onstage. Then he gave the upbeat. Ralph, Jackie and the string bassist, who were supplying the continuo accompaniment, came in dead on cue. Half a beat later, the chorus joined them.

Manny shook his head and, with a sharp gesture, cut off the sound.

"From the top," he said. Again Ralph, Jackie and the bassist did their thing. Again the chorus came in late.

"One more time," Manny said. Ralph and the others played their nice rich opening chord. This time, some of the choristers made it.

Most did not.

Manny let his arms drop to his sides. Slowly, wearily, like a toilworn farmer at the end of the day, he let his head sag and his shoulders slump. Several seconds ticked by. The last echo of the music died away.

"Ecco," Manny said silkily into the quiet. The balance of his address to the chorus, also in Italian, was not quiet. According to one of the oboists, who later translated its more vivid passages, Manny was inquiring of his audience why so completely motley a group of the illegitimate sons and daughters of the stray cats of Verona lacked even the elementary musicality of the cats their parents, to the point of a permanent and constitutional inability even to yowl on time.

The chorus looked interested, even impressed.

"Andiamo." Manny first rapped with his pencil, then waved it to set the music in motion. This time, there were no stragglers among the choristers and Manny kept them going on for eighty-four bars about the joys of pastoral disport.

For the first time since the rehearsal started, I could let myself relax, draw a deep breath and look around me, at the rows of columns along the sides of the nave, at the curve of the great wooden roof in the shadows overhead, at the enormous rose window in the west wall, at a huge vase of polished stone tucked away in a corner near the entrance.

I've played in scores of different places, from people's living rooms to office buildings to theater pits to Carnegie and Philharmonic Halls. In some, I've felt uncomfortable, in others, right at home. San Zeno was one of the right-at-home places. Although I'd never set foot in it before, it seemed familiar, and, for all its hugeness, friendly.

These blithe thoughts were rudely interrupted by a sudden stirring and scraping.

The chorus, its opening number over, disposed itself about the stage in the casual groupings befitting nymphs and shepherds. The muttered directions and ripe oaths of the stage manager died away.

It was time for Sabrina's first aria.

My heart bumped apprehensively once or twice as I watched

Ralph, Terry and Jackie get ready to play. Sabrina, I knew, was capable of anything. She could stand there on stage like a wooden dummy and yet sing flawlessly. Or she could act the part of the deserted Ariadne like a second Bernhardt but sing it like Miss Piggy in the shower.

Manny made sure Ralph & Company were watching and cocked his head for their upbeat. Sabrina, moving slowly downstage, folded her hands nicely over her tummy and began to sing. "*Ah! destino crudele* . . ."

She did it absolutely delightfully, both acting and singing. No fluffing, no fire-alarming, no sweeping gestures. The crucial high A was negotiated, the passagework conquered. And as she finished, Sabrina took her two steps forward, did her half turn and raised the hand she was supposed to raise in metaphoric farewell to Teseo, her departed lover, who had fled the scene well before the action of the opera begins.

Manny nodded appreciatively and kept the harpsichord, gamba and bass moving into the baritone recitative that came next.

Onstage, Sabrina pouted. She looked as if she expected Manny to stop the music just to rave about her performance. But at least she had enough presence to turn on cue and move gracefully upstage in her gauzy costume and out of the way of the burly baritone.

I caught her eye and mouthed "Terrific!" at her to cheer her up. She rewarded me with a big smile.

The opera rolled on. Nymphs appeared and sang. Lovelorn shepherds, singing, followed the nymphs around. Satyrs from the hills chased away the shepherds and made love to the nymphs. One of the satyrs tried to make love to Sabrina, but she sang him her second solo, to the effect that she was the betrothed of Teseo, the wretch, but that even though he, the thief of her heart, had basely deserted her, for which he would one day incur the vengeance of the gods and lose the woman he loved, she, Arianna, was still his betrothed and would never love another.

Her second solo wasn't as delicious as her first, but it was good enough to stymie the satyr. And David, accompanying her on theorbo, did a magnificent job, with rolled chords, arpeggiation, doubled trills, the lot.

"Hot hands! Gimme a high five, man!" he whispered, making like a basketball star while Manny waved the strings on into the little intermezzo that got Sabrina back in place upstage. I grinned, but I was too busy with my fiddle to grab at his hand.

At the start of the second act, Bacchus—at least I think it was Bacchus—announced to Sabrina in song that her prayers had been answered and that someday the wretch Teseo would be sorry he'd made her cry. Then Bacchus tried to make love to her, but he was distracted by some wild goings-on among the nymphs and satyrs, who now seemed to be called bassarids. Next, Silenus bawled a comic drinking song at the top of his basso lungs, with obbligato by one of Manny's oboists on oboe and Terry, rattling a tambourine.

Manny wasn't happy with Silenus and made him sing the number twice, but eventually we got on with it.

Sabrina, much taken with Silenus's jollity, decides in her third and last solo that she's foolish to mourn away her youth on behalf of the wretch Teseo, who after all is enjoying himself with other women right and left. Instead, she will repair to the hills with the nymphs and bassarids and do a little enjoying herself. Exit Sabrina, glancing flirtatiously over her shoulder. Exit Bacchus. Final chorus of nymphs and bassarids caroling that wine alone had the power to turn sadness into rejoicing in men's hearts. Thinking of the count, I devoutly hoped the librettist was right.

Then we were done. Manny went over his comments with us, scene by scene. The chorus clattered offstage and back to its bus. The principals disappeared chattering into the crypt to change out of their skimpy costumes. Moments later, they reappeared, crying aloud for coffee, tea, minestrone, anything hot. I could sympathize: San Zeno was decidedly chilly for bare arms and muslin-draped torsos.

David decided to ride back on the bus with Sabrina and meet us later at Wendy's.

Ralph, Terry and I put the quilted cover on Ralph's harpsichord and shifted it into the sacristy, where a small white-haired attendant vowed that he personally would protect it from all harm, even though the nights were cold and dark and, *signori*, I assure you though of course you will not believe me—that's what Ralph said he was saying—that more creatures walk in San Zeno at night than the good priests like to think about.

Jackie, all packed up, was waiting for us at the side entrance.

The four of us were turning the corner of Via San Giuseppe when I found myself staring at a pair of passersby walking in the opposite direction.

"Hey," I said.

"What's the problem?" Terry asked.

"That hat." The light could have been better, but I was almost positive. The hat had a Tyrolese narrow brim. The man wearing the hat, and also a shabby dark raincoat, was someone very familiar.

Well, why not? Verona is a small city.

But what was Commissario Ratner doing strolling and chatting in brotherly amiability with that smallish man in the gray sharkskin suit?

Again in dancing, one does not only observe
the measure of the music, but a measure
which is other than musical . . .

Cornazano,
Art of Dancing

CHAPTER ELEVEN

"His name is Reyes Garcia y Lopez," said Commissario Ratner.
"He is French."

"French?"

"Born in France, raised in France and"—the commissario
looked around his office uncomfortably and lowered his voice as
though repeating a joke he didn't want to be overheard repeating—"in prison in France."

I looked at him.

"That was years ago," he said. "Now Reyes Garcia is an important man in Verona. In all of the Veneto. Some people say he
owns a whole bank, the Credito Pietà. He has told me interesting things about you."

"About me?"

The commissario permitted himself a small smile of gratifica-
tion. "Mr. French, you have promised to assist us in our researches into a death by violence. Why have you not said anything of your business connection with Count Emilio
Sabinetti?"

"Is that the interesting thing this Reyes Garcia told you?" I
asked him. "Because if it is, you better get yourself another
source."

"Indeed? Then you deny that you visited Sabinetti in his office yesterday? With your friend Miss Craine?"

"Of course I don't deny it," I said grumpily. "Why should I? I
met *your* friend, the convicted lawbreaker Reyes Garcia, right
outside the count's door, and your friend Garcia, by the way,
scared the count's secretary out of her wits. But that doesn't

mean I consort with known criminals, any more than a visit to
the count means we're doing some kind of conspiracy."

Commissario Ratner actually laughed out loud. "Fair enough,
Mr. French," he said. "One visit does not necessarily mean a
. . . connection, I agree. But"—he eyed me shrewdly—"you
would hardly have gone to the count's office to discuss opera, I
presume."

"We did not discuss opera," I admitted with what I hoped was
a fine display of candor. It was time to put into play the sugges-
tion Jackie had made a couple of days earlier. "If you want, I'll
tell you what we did discuss. Let me see . . . It was Wednesday
night, and we were coming back from a picnic and we met the
count. And he seemed upset about something."

Ratner nodded.

"So the next morning Jackie—Miss Craine—and I called at his
office. He told us that he was sure Attilio was involved in some
evildoing and that had led to his death."

"Evildoing." Ratner savored the word. He shook his head.
"Attilio Caspardino? Evildoing is too strong a word, Mr.
French. We have information about sales of *cassoni*, antique
chests, that were not antique. There was a currency-smuggling
offense, but who in Italy has not at one time or another walked
across the frontier into Chiasso with a briefcase of lire? Doubt-
less there were other matters, of which we have not heard. The
worst thing we know of Attilio is that he was for a time a dealer
in cocaine—in a small way. Not on a scale grand enough to
make anyone murder him." Ratner shrugged. "So you see, Mr.
French, Sabinetti must have been referring to something other
than these affairs. Something we know nothing about." Again
he paused. I noted his use of "Sabinetti" rather than the more
respectful form of address. And I could tell from the careful lack
of expression on his face that he was cranking up to deliver a
surprise. "My friend Reyes Garcia thinks it had to do with
Sabinetti's business. Which is wine."

So that was it. "Could be," I said, "but the count didn't mention wine. Or anything else specific. Sorry."

"You are sure?"

Perhaps it was time for a delicate little flirtation with the truth, followed by a display of righteous American indignation. "The count says that he doesn't know what his cousin was involved in," I said assertively. "He says he thought his cousin might have wanted to talk to him about it, but that he never did." It didn't seem necessary to add that our dinner the night Attilio was murdered was to have been the setting for this conversation. "Now, Commissario. I don't mind being cooperative. I was happy to come in when you called. But tonight is the opening performance of the festival, and I have to get back to my work."

"You must rehearse?"

"Naturally."

"Tonight is what event?"

"*L'Arianna*. The opera."

"Hmm. Will there be a reception afterward?"

"I think so." In fact, I knew so.

"Will Sabinetti be there?" Ratner asked, in the next breath answering his own question. "Of course he will be there. He is this year's patron." For a moment, Ratner sat thinking. Then he said: "Mr. French, I should like you to ask Sabinetti a question, and then let me know his answer. Ask him . . . ask him if his cousin Attilio had ever offered to be *mediatore*, that is broker, to help him sell his wine."

"I think you should ask the count yourself," I said.

Ratner began to look annoyed. "I want *you* to ask him," he said shortly. "He will not be so defensive in his answer. And it is important to know."

"Why is it so important?" I asked.

"Excuse me, because I tell you it is," Ratner snapped. He added more calmly, "We think it will speed matters up if we can establish a business as well as a blood relationship between Sabinetti and the cousin. But that is all I wish to say on the subject. Ask the question, Mr. French, if you please, that is all." He sat back and ran a hand over his neatly brushed black hair. "I would offer you coffee," he said, "but, unfortunately . . ." He gestured at the pile of dossiers on his desk.

"I understand," I said, only too glad to get out of there.

Outside, the sun was bright, the morning traffic was brisk and it was a relief to realize that my fellow pedestrians would not be drawing away because I smelled sour, like a police informer.

"I still want to know who the hell this Reyes Garcia is," I said plaintively to Jackie a few minutes later.

She shook her head, turned back to the fountain with the water coming out of the lion's mouth and went on washing the huge fresh peaches we'd just bought from a market stand in the Piazza Erbe.

"If your mouth wasn't so full, you could help me figure it out," I said.

She sat by my side on the edge of the stone trough. Her tongue crept out and licked up a fragment of peach caught at the side of her mouth. She smiled. "I can tell you all about Reyes Garcia," she said.

"You can?"

"I can, and do you know how? Because while you were out keeping your appointment with that Inspector Ratner—"

"Commissario Ratner."

"—I was eating breakfast with the count, and I asked him."

"What did he say?"

"I asked him who the man was who had stopped us on the way out of his office. At first, he didn't want to talk about him. But then he told me his name, Garcia y something, like a cigar—"

"Lopez," I said.

"—and that he was a banker and a man of influence. I think I was supposed to believe that he was the head of the Verona branch of the Mafia."

"He very well could be," I said.

"You're kidding. No," she said, looking at me carefully, "you're not kidding."

"Well, he's done time," I said.

"Wonderful," Jackie said. "Emilio never told me that."

"Garcia apparently told Ratner that we were up to our ears in deals with your buddy Emilio," I said. "He also tipped off

Ratner that Cousin Attilio's murder might have something to do with wine."

"Oh, dear," Jackie said. She had her hair in braids and she was wearing those white short shorts I had strictly forbidden her to wear anywhere public in Italy and she was distracting me.

"And not only that," I said. "Ratner wants me to find out more about Attilio and the count and tell him all about it. I hate being a fink."

"You're not one at all," Jackie said. "You're doing it to help Emilio, not get him arrested. Besides, if you didn't do it, that Ratner would stick you in jail. He said so himself."

"That's all true," I said, "but I still hate it."

"At least stop brooding about it," Jackie said.

"What *should* I brood about?" I asked her.

"You could start brooding about how you and Terry are going to get to the Motor Hotel Ortofrutticolo, meet the Yugoslavs, get the samples and get back in time for the concert."

"I already have," I said. "I'm going to take a cab and have it wait."

"That's crazy," Jackie said. "It will cost a fortune."

"Maybe, but it's the best way."

"Why don't you ask the count to let Mauro drive you?"

"I thought of it," I said, "but I don't want Mauro to find out who we're doing business with or where. And I don't want our Yugoslavian friends to find out that the buyer is really Emilio Sabinetti."

"I guess you'll have to take a cab," Jackie agreed. As unofficial treasurer of the Antiqua Players, she was pained by the expense, I knew.

"Tell you what," I said. "If the price is higher than seventy-six thousand lire, I'll send the cab away."

"Seventy-six thousand lire, that's about forty dollars."

"I guess so," I said.

"Okay. But if it's any more—"

"How about passing me one of those apricots?"

For a couple of heartbeats, with the taste of the apricot in my mouth and its juice running down my chin, and with Jackie's half-smiling face filling my vision, I was completely, idiotically happy. Then, reality reasserted itself and I was back in the world of music festivals, wine and sudden death.

"How does this Garcia know what we're doing with the count?" I said, half aloud. "And if he does know, why should he care? Unless . . ."

"Unless what?"

Strange ideas were beginning to bubble in my brain, about a man with a Spanish name who was French by birth and an Italian banker by trade.

"Forget it," I said. "It's too complicated for my crumbling mind to comprehend. I have to try to think. And you," I added, "are not making the job any easier."

In fact, three or four of the fruit vendors had deserted their stands and taken up a group position near the fountain, from which they were eyeing Jackie with passionate and vocal interest.

Jackie glanced up, caught sight of her fan club and blushed. "They don't mean anything by it," she said.

"That's right," I said. "They are just children. Or detached, clinical observers. Their desire to sample you like a glass of the count's finest stems solely from scientific curiosity." I moved closer and put a protective arm around her.

Laughter and cheers from the fan club.

"You have an appointment, don't forget," Jackie warned me.

"In half an hour. There's time to walk you back to the palazzo," I said. I drew a deep breath and squeezed harder.

"Do these fits come on you suddenly?" Jackie asked, a little out of breath herself. We were wandering slowly down a cobbled *vicolo* toward Sant'Anastasio and our home away from home.

"Only when you're here and instead of being with you I have to go do something trivial, like fight off a commissario and work on a million-dollar wine deal."

"Oh, Alan, you're sweet," she said, curling around to give me a little soft kiss.

"Oh, now! You stop that, now! You hear?"

I cut short a much more serious kiss.

It was Sabrina, of course, giving vent in her native accents to some not so jocular references to our behavior.

"Jesus!" I murmured between clenched teeth. "Someday I'll murder that little airhead."

"Hush, she's not little," Jackie said, "and she can hear you."

"How I wish she could," I said, "but she can't. Hello, Sabrina, dear, how are you?" I added much more loudly. "All set for your big night? I can feel it. You're going to be a star." I knew that would get to her. Singers are even more superstitious than actors. Mere mention of a performance that hadn't yet happened would be sure to drive Miss Sabrina Englander straight up the wall.

To my utter delight, Sabrina's mischievous smirk gave way to alarm.

"Don't you dare say another word!" she said quickly, backpedaling out of our way.

"I won't if you won't," I said.

Sabrina nodded, said something in a muffled voice about needing more throat spray and hurried away, presumably to buy some.

Terry was waiting at the entrance to the palazzo.

With the help of Orlando, we summoned a cab and entered into negotiations with the driver.

"He says the Ortofrutticolo is far beyond the railroad," Orlando translated warningly. "He says he will charge you *due volte.*"

"Tell him we are not children or tourists," I said.

Orlando and Jackie both laughed, seriously weakening our bargaining position. But after protracted discussion, a contract was ratified, the initial fee proffered and accepted and we climbed aboard.

"You guys be careful," Jackie said.

"I promise," I said.

"And be back by six. We have to be at San Zeno by seven."

The driver looked at Jackie, grinned wickedly and called something to her out the window as we pulled away from the curb. I had no idea what the words were, but the manner, as Doris Day sang in one of her golden oldies, was familiar.

Mercantia is a dance which is appropriately named.
One lady only dances with three men, and she gives
audience to all . . . as though she were a
merchant of love.

Cornazano,
Art of Dancing

CHAPTER TWELVE

Five minutes saw us clear of the old city and working our way
through heavy traffic into the belt of grimy industrial suburbs to
the south. From the scenery, I expected the Motor Hotel
Ortofrutticolo to be a bleak cement-block fortress right across
from Verona's huge produce market, a place where farmers and
truck drivers could snatch a few hours of sleep on gray sheets
before getting on with their unloading.

Wrong again, Alan French.

The Motor Hotel Ortofrutticolo was indeed across from the
produce market. But among its lesser amenities were espaliered
peach trees, a shaven lawn and, its glittering wavelets just visible through a wall of hollow sunscreen tiles, a monster swim-
ming pool.

"Too much," Terry murmured as we drew up to the entrance.

"Too much is not enough," I assured him.

Imagine a vast wood-and-glass A-frame with a two-story mar-
ble-floored lobby and a registration desk tiled in deep lavender
and you have the merest outline of the picture. The place made
even the biggest Ramada Inn look like a chicken coop. Everything that could be carpeted was carpeted, and everything that
couldn't be carpeted was either a mosaic or a mirror.

The gentleman at the desk, languidly consulting a register
bound in lavender leather, informed us that guests Miklaus and
Stavica awaited us in Room 330.

The corridor down which we strode toward Room 330 had
thirteen-foot ceilings. It was also about four miles long, which

allowed us ample opportunity to review our tactics. By the time
we reached the room door, panting slightly, we'd agreed not to
allow these representatives of the noncapitalist way to push us
around or hoodwink us into anything premature.

"And remember," I said to Terry, "if they try to get us drunk,
just say we've got to play tonight. And don't look at me like that,
they might try."

"Sure, boss, whatever you say."

I pushed the ivory button in the wall by the door. Chimes
sounded within and a few seconds later the door was flung open.

"Well, hi! For Chrissakes come on in!"

Whatever I'd expected our Yugoslav sample bearers to be, it
wasn't a twenty-year-old blond kid in a T-shirt and leather vest
and his girlfriend, also blond, wearing the Young Communist
uniform of tank top and jeans.

"This is really terrific!" the kid went on. "You must be Mr.
French, am I right? And this other guy is Mr. Monza. Sit down,
sit down, just move that stuff off the chair. I'm Petar and this is
Vivi, we just got here ourselves and I have to tell you, this is a
real pleasure!"

In whatever brief span they'd been there, Petar and Vivi had
managed to scramble Room 330 into a scene of total confusion.
The bed was as rumpled as if a gymnastics team had been using
it for a practice trampoline. Vivi's bright red canvas carryall
was open on one dresser. Spilling out of it was a heap of costume jewelry, a chewed-on gold pencil, a wad of ten-thousand-
lire notes, the large economy size of Giorgio perfume and a
canister of chemical Mace. Still inside was a small bundle of
wispy lingerie.

On the other dresser, a Japanese ghetto box was softly invok-
ing Italian rock. The big color television was turned to a dubbed
version of what I could identify as "Dallas," but the sound, mer-
cifully, had been turned all the way down.

Bottles and glasses were everywhere.

My stunned expression made Vivi giggle. "Hey, man," she
said, "I bet you think this is really far out." Her English was
barely accented, even if the turn of phrase was quaint.

"Crazy," I agreed.

"Well, everything's gonna be all reet," she said, putting her hands on her hips and swinging her torso from side to side to the beat of the radio, "because we got just what you want."

"You bet we do!" Petar echoed enthusiastically, "and here it is!" He reached into a fat leather satchel lying on the huge double bed and pulled out a box lined in plastic bubble wrap that held two clear screw-top wine bottles. Each bottle bore a typewritten label and each was filled with white wine. "You wanna try it?"

I started to say no—what do I know about tasting wine?—but Terry overruled me. "Yeah, let's check it out," he said.

From somewhere, Vivi produced two small paper cups. Petar poured and Vivi, smiling gaily, handed Terry and me samples of the sample, saying, "Now you will taste what *good* wine is like!"

For all their bounce, Vivi and Petar eyed us closely as we sniffed and made ready to sip. Petar's face looked suddenly less boyish, and Vivi stopped boogieing around and stood still.

Terry held the cup under his nose and inhaled deeply. "Very flowery," he said, *"molto fiorito.* A Traminer, huh?"

"No, no, no," Petar said. "Only a little flowery at first, when the bottle is opened. Not a Traminer, a Welschriesling, just what you ordered. Only to make it good and dry, we stuck in a little special wine, a Smederevka, with the Welschriesling."

"Tastes okay," Terry said, after gargling a small swig like mouthwash. "Tastes good."

"Good? It's wonderful!" Vivi exclaimed. "Nothing tastes better than our premium wines."

The commercial aside, I thought the wine smelled and tasted fine, but Terry put on a display of looking dubious. "I think it's okay," he said, "but we have to talk to our main man."

"Talk to *who?*"

"He means the, er, senior partner in our enterprise," I cut in. "But don't worry. We'll decide quickly. Possibly within a day."

"Today, even?"

I couldn't understand why Vivi, who was so eager to sell us the wine, would be disappointed that we might be ready to buy right away. But then I looked around the motel room and realized why: Vivi was enjoying herself. She didn't want their little Italian holiday to be over too soon.

"Probably not today," I said. "Maybe tomorrow."

She brightened immediately. "Then tonight we can have a blast," she said. "You will come back later and we'll all drink a lot of wine."

"Sounds good," said Terry.

"Fine," I said, screwing the lid on the open sample bottle and stuffing it with its fellow back in the plastic bag. "But first we've got to take the samples to our partner."

"Sure, sure," Petar said amiably. "You get the word, you call us. We'll be right here."

"What's all the other wine for?" Terry asked as we were leaving.

"Different wines of our country," Vivi said, "for us to drink together when you come back. With an order," she added emphatically. "I'm thirsty, too, so hurry!"

The bottles in the bag chinking companionably, we hurried back down the corridor to the lobby.

"Think it'll be okay?" I asked Terry.

"Who knows?" he said shrewdly. "You don't want to think too much right now."

The sunlight made us blink, but it wasn't hot enough to have melted our taxicab into a grease splotch on the pavement. Still, a grease splotch was all we found when we stepped outside.

Terry and I looked at each other.

"I'll try to get another one," I began. But I never finished the sentence.

Three men came up behind us, blocking our way back into the lobby. One of them was at least as large as the missing taxi. The others were more normal in size, and clearly no match for us. That is, either one of them could have taken care of both of us. And it looked more and more as if that was exactly what they had in mind.

"Hey, you," the big man grunted in English. "Come here."

"Me?" I said, stalling.

They spread out and began moving slowly toward us. I looked around for help. There was nobody there. "Help," I said in conversational tones.

The human taxi laughed. "Give us the wine, you," he said.

"*Help!*" I screamed as loudly as I could.

Still nobody.

"Aw, shit!" Terry muttered. "At least lemme have a bottle."

"Take one," I said, shoving it at him. Then the human taxi was upon me. *In that checked cap, he even looks like a taxi*, I thought wildly. A hand like a ham just grazed my nose. Leaping frantically backward, I stumbled into somebody who mouthed a rich Italian oath. We both sat down hard on the Ortofrutticolo's driveway, but the other guy, I was happy to feel, sat down harder.

"*Gli esempi!*" I thought I heard somebody shout.

There was a sharp crack in my ear followed by a shrill yelp and a whole volley of oaths, then the sound of another blow and then the wiry arm encircling my throat suddenly went slack and the knee left off gouging my spine.

Cautiously, I sat up. The bottle in my hand was still intact.

A few feet away, Terry, clutching the other sample bottle, stood breathing heavily. He was bleeding slightly from a cut on his cheek.

The human taxi and the thug who had been doing the number on Terry were rounding the corner of the motel at speed.

In the gutter beside me, moaning, lay the gentleman from whom I'd just disentangled myself.

"There! I knew there was some funny thing happening!" It was Vivi, slightly disheveled, her eyes blazing and her Americanese slipping badly. "What a good thing we came to see!" In Vivi's hand was a small but serious-looking automatic. "I am glad I have to shoot no one, only hit with the gun. But I would have!"

I believed her.

Wordlessly, Petar approached Terry and reached out a hand for the bottle of wine. Terry gave it to him. "Unbelievable," he breathed.

"Yes, isn't it fantastic?" Petar agreed. "It's not broken, it's not even cracked." He turned it over to me.

"Now . . . you!" Vivi said.

Her victim, gray-faced, had risen to his hands and knees before vomiting conclusively on the pavement. Vivi pushed him with the toe of her running shoe and he collapsed with a mournful sigh. It's obviously no fun at all to be pistol-whipped, even by a pretty girl.

"I will go inside and call the police to take him away," Vivi said. She dropped her gun into her carryall and walked sedately back into the lobby.

Petar looked at us thoughtfully. "What's this all about?"

"I have no idea," I said. "Muggers, I suppose."

"No way, man." Petar's command of the idiom was more durable than Vivi's. "Muggers don't go after people in broad daylight, and anyway no rich tourists come here. Those types were after *you*. Have you done something bad to somebody?"

Only Commissario Ratner and Signor Reyes Garcia y Lopez. Nobody important.

"No," I lied.

"Well, it's none of my business," Petar said, "but maybe you should be taking better care of yourselves."

"We'll try to do that," I said, "and . . . thanks."

"The good salesman looks after his customers," Petar said. "We're only being good salesmen."

"Believe me, we appreciate it," I said.

Vivi returned, once more artlessly cheerful. "I called the cops," she said. "But *first* I called a taxi. He should be here—ah . . ."

As she spoke, a taxicab pulled up to the entrance.

"Go back to your hotel," Petar said rapidly. "We will deal with the police. No sense in you getting involved."

"Well, thank you for that, too," I said. "We'll telephone you later today or tomorrow morning."

"Come back tonight," Vivi called. "We'll drink wine."

Oh sure.

We climbed wearily into the cab and I gave the driver the

address. At least I had the sense not to let Vivi and Petar over-hear it.

Terry slumped back in his seat and flexed his fingers. "My hands are okay," he said, "but the rest of me—"

"I know just how you feel," I said. My tailbone ached from its encounter with cement, my neck was sore from my assailant's choke hold and my energy level was off the low side of the dial.

"Who *were* those guys?" Terry demanded.

"I don't know for sure," I admitted. "But if they are who I think they could be, they got what they were after."

"What do you mean?"

"Information. Listen." I leaned closer to him, wincing at the ache in my poor neck muscles. "I think those goons were Reyes Garcia's. I think Garcia is tracking us to see what we do. He knows we're playing in the festival. But like I was telling Jackie earlier, he knows there's something more, something to do with wine. I don't *think* he knows what. But he follows us out to the motel—"

"Probably he owned the cabbie."

"Could be. But anyway, what would a couple of musicians be doing in a motel in this part of town? Well, now his thugs can tell him part of the answer. We were meeting someone about wine."

"If you're right," Terry said, "we're in deep shit."

"And getting deeper." I thought for a moment and glanced at my watch. "It's four o'clock."

"Jesus. We have to play tonight."

"We've got until six. The first thing we do when we get back is give these samples to the count."

"Right," Terry agreed. "And hang around while he checks them out."

"The next thing—"

"The next thing is to get together with David and Ralph and Jackie and warn them," Terry interrupted. "I don't want those characters anywhere near any of us."

"For sure," I said. "And the third thing is to get ahold of Vivi and Petar and tell them to move."

"You think?" Terry said. "They can take care of themselves."
"Maybe," I said.

But when we got back to the palazzo, after being hung up for ten minutes in nightmarish traffic near the Arena, Orlando greeted me with a note delivered just a few minutes earlier: "See you at the Hotel Giusti, Love, P & V."

"See what I mean?" Terry said. "They got the message."

"A very good hotel, *signor*," said Orlando, "on the Via Carducci. And, yes," he said in answer to my question, "it's quite safe."

I banged on Jackie's door. When she answered, I told her what had happened.

Her response was not what you'd call supportive. "Why didn't you just give them the bottles and run?" she asked.

"There wasn't time," I said, "and besides—"

"—and besides, we couldn't just let them get away with it," she finished my sentence for me. She grabbed me and kissed me hard. Then she let go and said: "You macho men. When will you ever learn?"

"But, Jackie—"

"I am not Lois Lane," she said. "I get no kick out of bloodshed."

"But you still want us to go ahead and do what we can for the count," I argued.

"I guess so," Jackie said. "Only with your brain, not your brawn." She promised to find Ralph and David and to keep the three of them indoors and out of trouble while Terry and I went in search of the count.

The count saw us at once. "You have the samples?" he said, closing the door to his office.

I handed him the bag with the two bottles in it.

"You have tested these yourself? What do you think? No, no, you are right, of course, don't tell me." He poured himself a sample, lowered his big patrician nose into the glass, sniffed once and repeated exactly what Terry had said: "It's flowery, like a German wine. But wait . . ." A few seconds later, he sniffed again. "The flowery bouquet is *much* less prominent," he said with a smile. "The taste is acceptable, not a Sauvignon but close to a Riesling-Italiano, not as peppery as a Garganega . . . Where is it from?"

I shook my head.

"Of course," said the count, still smiling. "You wish to keep your secret. I think I know it, but I will not inquire. If we can get rid of the *fiorituro*, gentlemen, and I think we can by oxygenating, then . . . I will buy this wine. You will leave the samples with me? I will give you a receipt and we will talk again tonight at the reception. Okay?" He took out a silver pen and quickly wrote us a receipt.

"One more thing," I said.

"What is that, Mr. French?"

"Why is your friend Signor Reyes Garcia so interested in us?"

The count's smile tightened. "Is he interested? If he is, I cannot say why. But Signor Garcia is not a good person to offend."

"I'm sure you're right," I said. "We're doing our damnedest to stay out of his way. Perhaps a certain amount of discretion about this wine would help us."

"Signor Garcia is active on my behalf. But I will try to do as you wish."

"We'll see you later, then."

"*Arrivederla*, gentlemen."

You must have Memory so as to remember the steps
you are about to perform when you begin to dance.
Cornazano,
Art of Dancing

CHAPTER THIRTEEN

San Zeno looked magnificent. To Manny Gardi's astonishment
—"What's wrong? what's wrong?" he kept asking—the five of us
made the bus and the six o'clock rehearsal, which was just a
brushup of a few of the trickier instrumental passages. So we
started in the empty church, broke for half an hour to drink
broth in Styrofoam cups and eat thin sandwiches in the cloister
(by permission of the very nervous verger) and stood behind the
hangings that defined the performing area to watch the beautiful nave, half lit by the spring sunshine, fill up with people.

"I'm still hungry," David said.

"Go out and get yourself something," Jackie said. "You've got
twenty minutes."

"Oh, well, I can wait," he said. But a minute later, when I
turned to look for him, he was gone.

"Back to the *tavola calda*," Terry said with a shrug.

Terry and I, being woodwind players, eat very little before
concerts. There's nothing like a hearty meal to turn the old
tummy muscles treacherous and screw up your breathing and
phrasing.

"Actually, it's the diaphragm, not the stomach," said Jackie.

"What do you care, you're a fiddler," I said. "You never do eat
before you play anyway, but it wouldn't matter if you gorged
yourself."

"Eating distracts the mind," Jackie said.

"Not eating distracts it more," Terry said.

"How can you people even *think* about food?" Ralph said,
shuddering visibly. Over his white tie and tails, Ralph was wearing a full-length down coat suitable for Antarctic exploration.

On his hands were the sealskin mittens we'd bought him the previous Christmas. Despite all of this, he was shivering sporadically as if he had a fever.

Stage fright.

We all suffer from it, but Ralph is truly one of the afflicted.

"Have you found it?" Jackie asked him.

Ralph nodded. "It's through that archway," he whispered.

About ten minutes before every performance, Ralph will head for the nearest toilet and be miserably, retchingly sick. He's tried pills, he's tried therapy, but it always happens. All we can do is sympathize. And thank God that it doesn't happen to us.

Manny Gardi came by in *his* formal attire. "It's a hell of a house," he said. "It's the beginning of the season and the Arena isn't going and who ever heard of Jacopo di Preti, and still the place is jumping." He looked absolutely delighted, and who could blame him? Conducting to a half-empty hall is not one of music's happier experiences.

Jackie surveyed him critically. "Hold still," she commanded, moving in on him. "Your tie is crooked."

"So young to be so aggressive," Manny said with a grin.

"She does it to all of us," I said.

"It's a good thing I do," Jackie said, tugging at the white linen. "Otherwise you'd all look like Red O'Brien's Rockland Serenaders."

"Who?" Manny said incredulously.

The Serenaders, I informed him, was a local dance band straight out of the 1940s, consisting of two trumpets, two saxes, a clarinetist who doubled on flute for the Latin numbers, guitar, piano, bass and drums. Jackie and I had found Red and his boys one Saturday night last summer, when, in pursuit of adventure, we'd strayed northward into the New York hinterland and pulled up at a log cabin roadhouse on the way to nowhere. Entranced, we'd swung and swayed to their rhythms all evening. They were long on Brylcreme but short on technique.

"God! I promise to learn how to tie my tie straight."

"That's much better," Jackie said, giving his cheek a pat. "Break a leg."

"On this podium, it could easily happen," Manny said and went off on some last-minute errand.

David reappeared. "I gob a goob gub yum," he said with his mouth still full. "Wab sub?"

"Sounds delicious," Jackie said, "but no thanks."

The overhead lights blinked. This supposedly gave us two minutes before we took our places. About half the members of the chorus, now in appropriate attire, were shuffling around, hawking and spitting and otherwise readying themselves to sing. The rest of them were still out in their bus, ingesting controlled substances, making and giggling at obscene wisecracks and in general behaving like choristers.

"Excuse me," said Ralph. He fled through the fatal archway to the *gabinetto*. I followed and waited outside. There were the usual noises within. About a minute passed before Ralph emerged, deathly pale but functioning.

"Mint?" I said. Jackie makes me keep a roll of them for him.

He took one and nodded his thanks. Then he slipped out of his down coat, hung it over a chair, flicked at his tie and lined up with the rest of us.

Manny Gardi signaled us with a wink and a jerk of the head and, to mild applause, we filed out to our places.

We went through the ritual of shoving the chairs around and fussing with instruments and equipment. The stone flooring of San Zeno isn't designed for music stands, but a little fast work with wedges of paper took care of the inevitable wobbles. We tuned up.

Then the applause grew stronger and Manny came striding out, tails flapping in the breeze. Manny, bless his heart, dispenses with the usual conductorial posturing and preening. Almost as soon as he reached the podium, up went his stick to launch us on the overture.

It went okay: a little uneven in spots and a little off key, but nothing on which a critic could really sharpen his meat-ax. Midway through the final strain, I heard the scuffling behind the curtain that told me the chorus was assembling. But no stampings or mumbled imprecations reached my ear, so I assumed that at least a working majority had made it onstage, and when I had time to look up from my music I found I was right.

The chorus, too, sounded bright. Manny's emphatic baton kept it under reasonable control. While the boys and girls told us and told us again what fun it was to mind the sheep, I felt myself start to sit back comfortably and relax, all ready for an evening of music-making.

The chorus finished. Okay, Sabrina.

To the buttery sound of harpsichord, bass recorder and gamba, she glided downstage like the princess she was supposed to be. The lighting super tracked her with a small spotlight. It made her brown tresses shine prettily: she must have remembered to wash her hair. Sabrina brought her hands together at her waist. Her lungs filled. Her lips parted.

Nothing came out.

Cold sweat broke out on my brow.

I could see Manny's baton waver uncertainly at the bottom of the downbeat. Instinctively, I tightened my grip on the neck of my violin and half raised my bow. But of course there was nothing I could do.

For a split second, Sabrina stood there, voiceless and helpless, a victim of total catastrophe. Then it registered on her as it registered on me that the music, somehow, had never faltered.

Ralph.

Without turning a hair or skipping a note, Ralph had kept on going, playing straight through the missed cue to the end of the strophe, nodding emphatically to keep the others with him, smiling encouragement at Sabrina, lifting a hand from the keyboard to turn a page of the score.

I *know* Ralph and what Ralph can do and I still had trouble identifying the imperturbable figure at the harpsichord with the pallid, unsteady bundle of wretchedness who'd crept out of the john a few moments earlier.

Now he was starting a reprise of Sabrina's introduction, bringing the theme around again, this time elaborating on it, improvising embellishments, first making it an elegant little variation for harpsichord and then an excuse for some bravura passagework.

For a bar or so, Jackie and Terry could only chase after Ralph, but then they caught up. Manny, too, fell off the back of the beat and had to struggle to recover. They managed to get together quickly enough to keep the audience fooled. But in four more bars Sabrina would have to start singing. Otherwise, the game was really over.

Ralph's lips moved. I had no idea what he was saying. But Sabrina heard. She nodded slightly in response. The stricken-deer expression left her face. She even smiled. And right on cue, as if absolutely nothing had gone wrong, she began to sing about cruel Destiny.

My heart started to beat again.

Terry, the bass recorder robbing him of speech, kept on playing but rolled his eyes eloquently.

Sabrina was caroling away, her head tilted back slightly, her eyes half closed in concentration. Fascinated as always, I watched the muscles of her mouth and throat pulse and relax, her chest lift evenly with each intake of breath. Her face flushed. Perspiration formed at her temples and trickled like unheeded tears down her face, down her neck. Don't ever kid yourself, singers work hard. But in the middle of all that exercise, Sabrina kept her articulation and phrasing steady and didn't force her held notes. She was singing, not being the noon whistle in a boiler factory.

Good girl, I thought, then laughed to myself at how furious Sabrina always was when anyone called her a girl. Okay, then, good woman. But in music, you can't just prove one thing and stop. The music keeps on going. You have to keep on climbing mountains, all the way to the end.

Sabrina made the high A. She polished off her first cadence and held her pose through the instrumental *ritornello*. I watched her closely. I knew she was wondering: Can I do it all again?

She set herself solidly on those long sturdy legs and gave a determined little toss of her head. And then she did do it all again. I felt like cheering.

At long last—it seemed like a week since she'd missed that first cue—the number was over. Then, thank God, came a good round of applause, a *bravo!* or two and a chance for Sabrina to stop waving to Teseo and take a bow before the baritone moved in.

We were fifteen minutes into a ninety-minute performance. I had barely warmed up my bowing arm and hadn't so much as touched the flute, and I was already as limp as a leftover dim sum dumpling.

Fortunately, the rest of the first act went along, as they say, without incident. Sabrina brought off her second solo, the one about still being engaged to Teseo, with enough bounce to make up for a couple of off-key high notes. And David's theorbo act charmed the audience.

They'd curtained off half of one of the aisles for us to use during intermission. Jackie and I arrived there slightly ahead of the hero of the hour.

"O-o-o-o, Ralph, oh my sweet darlin', oh!" Sabrina, sobbing, flung herself at him like somebody running for a bus, her accent pure corn pone. "You're so wonderful, you're just humongous!"

Ralph's knees buckled slightly but he bore up well under the assault. "Now, take it easy," he said soothingly. "A little mistake like that could happen to anybody." Over Sabrina's shoulder, he grinned at us. He was enjoying himself hugely.

"But it happened to me!" Sabrina wailed. "And you saved me! I'll never, I swear, I'll never forget it!"

Manny Gardi came through the archway from the john. His face and hair were still dripping from the water he'd poured over himself.

He slapped Ralph on the back. "By God," he said heartily, "I thought we'd had it that time! But you bailed us out. Terrific job. You, too, young lady," he said to Jackie. "Damn glad all of you people are with us.

"And as for you"—her rounded jovially on Sabrina—"you've got a lot of guts, drying like that and then coming back. I know plenty who couldn't have done it. Big names, too. Here, put something around yourself and find a place to sit down. There's a lot more of this thing to go and we want you in good shape."

"If you all will excuse me," Sabrina said, detaching herself from Ralph as soon as Manny moved away, "I think I will sit down." But a couple of minutes later, she was grabbing eagerly at the arm of Fritz the Swiss, the tenor who was singing Bacchus.

"Is she going to make it all the way through?" I asked Jackie.

"Christus! I hope so!"

"She'll make it," Ralph said drily. "I'm not so sure about Fritz."

But Fritz was razor-sharp in the *arietta* which opened the second act, the nymphs and satyrs capered about with suitable abandon, Silenus rolled and roared and Sabrina herself did a sprightly job on the subject of pleasuring herself in the hills. I played lead violin in the little second-act overture and a couple of intermezzi and got in my licks on the flute. Almost before we knew it, act two was over and Manny and the cast were taking curtain calls.

As the patron of the *festivale*, Count Emilio himself went up front to bow.

"Boy, does he look not happy," Terry said. I had to agree with him. The count was as elegant as ever, but under the bright lights his face was tired and his smile seemed strained.

Seeing him jerked my attention away from music and back to reality. Reality became no cheerier when Terry jogged my elbow. "Look who's here," he said.

No more than fifteen yards away, amid a group of prosperous-looking citizens, was Reyes Garcia. With him was a slender, dark-haired girl in a beige dress. She stood quietly by as Garcia chatted with his neighbors.

"She can't be any more than sixteen," I muttered disapprovingly at Garcia. "Shame on you."

"Yeah," Terry said, "some guys have all the luck."

The crowd was starting to thin out, and in a moment Garcia and his companion, with the rest of their party, were making their way toward the door.

I took apart my wooden flute, ran a brush through the bore, wrapped the flute carefully in a worn black velvet cloth and tucked it away. Then I turned my attention to my violin and bow and music. The others, too, were packing up. We were all too tired and drained to say much about the performance. That would come later.

By the time Manny Gardi stopped by to say thanks, San Zeno was almost empty. I was grateful for the quiet dimness.

Jackie sat next to me on the bus and squeezed my hand.

"All I want, in this order," I said, "is a drink, a hot bath and a twenty-minute snooze."

"And what about me?"

I decided to risk reprisal. "First you can scrub my back, then you can watch me sleep."

"I *knew* there was a place for me in your life."

In actual fact, when we got back to the palazzo I was the one who got the drinks and ran the bath and scrubbed Jackie's back, and we both stretched out on the bed.

"I thought you wanted to take a nap," Jackie said after a minute.

"I do," I said.

"But?" she said, her body moving slowly under my hand.

"Some things in life are more important than sleep."

"Oh, yes, I do agree," she whispered.

Nobody knocked on the door and nobody called on the phone and the closed shutters held the night sounds of the city at bay, and after not too long we did fall asleep.

He who wishes to see the heavens open, let him
experience the beneficence of Duke Borso.

Cornazano,
Art of Dancing

CHAPTER FOURTEEN

The warmth, the babble of voices, the clinking of glasses and the
flickering light of scores of candles all made my head spin
slightly. I'd coaxed Jackie into bare red silk and earrings for the
count's reception, and heads turned as we made our way
through the crowd near the bar. They turned only briefly,
though: enough female flesh was on display that evening to
make head-turning a waste of male energy.

"Wow!" Jackie suddenly said under her breath. She held my
arm more tightly.

"What's the matter?"

"Over there. Look!"

I looked.

At the center of one of the biggest and liveliest knots of people in the room stood Sabrina. In the bare-flesh sweepstakes, she
was clearly out to be the all-time winner. Her black dress began
by leaving absolutely nothing to the imagination, and as she
turned smilingly from one admirer to another the spillage from
her bodice became more and more a matter of grave international concern.

"Dar-leeng!" I heard one woman exclaim solicitously, dab-
bing with a wispy handkerchief at the perspiration on her upper
lip. "Such a triumph! How wonderful you were! But you must
be freezing! Do be careful not to catch cold!"

"Why, I'm just a little old country gal," Sabrina answered
gaily. "A little itty-bitty breeze isn't going to hurt me. Is it,
Massimo honey?"

Jackie and I were giggling so hard that we never did hear

what Massimo honey, face flushed above a silver bow tie, said in reply.

A quick look around reassured us that our fellow Antiqua Players were satisfactorily occupied. David we saw seated on a bench comfortably out of the rush of traffic. Deep in conversation with him was a smashing blonde in an emerald dress. Between them on the bench were a whole flask of wine and two plates heaped high with hors d'oeuvre. They paid no attention whatever to the ancestral portrait that glowered disapprovingly down at them from the wall.

Ralph, resplendent in a canary-yellow dinner jacket, murmured something to Jackie as he passed by on his way out.

"He's off to a little dinner," she said. "I think he said it was at Prince Espoglioso's, but it might have been Princess Somebody Else's."

"A title on the door rates at least half the guests on the floor," I said.

Terry materialized beside us. "The count really knows how to throw a blast, huh?" he said. "I think I'll check out that babe over near Manny Gardi."

"Which one?"

"The one in the tan dress. I think she sings in the chorus. See you later."

"And don't call her a babe," said Jackie to his departing back.

For the next half hour, we ate and drank and wandered about.

As elaborate as it was, the count's reception was a typical postperformance affair. That is, the nonmusician guests mostly herded together and fraternized with one another, totally ignoring the musicians, who were left to fend for themselves. The fascinated circle surrounding Sabrina, we decided, was only the exception that proved the rule.

"Looks like we're going to be an exception, too," I said.

Count Emilio himself, his faced creased in a welcoming smile, was edging toward us and shepherding another couple with him.

"It was a fantastic performance, eh?" he greeted us. "That girl . . . fantastic! But, please. Allow me to present Frank and Ellie

Fisher. The Fishers are countrymen of yours, from Montclair in New Jersey. Ellie, Frank, Alan French is head of his own splendid group, the Antiqua Players, and this is Miss Jackie Craine, who plays the viola da gamba so superbly."

Frank Fisher was one of those tall, rangy frosty-haired types in their fifties that ad agency talent directors like to cast as executives in commercials for banks, brokerage houses and upscale merchandise. His handshake was firm but friendly, his gaze was sincere and there were laugh wrinkles at the corners of his eyes. Frank Fisher made me want to work hard at the office, massage my gums nightly and otherwise qualify as his friend.

In her way, Ellie Fisher was just as perfect. Her eyes, too, had laugh lines at their corners, and she made no effort to hide them. She was still as slim as a young girl, and she was slipping into middle age as gracefully as she would slip into the elegant fur wrap around her shoulders.

"Jackie?" she said in a quiet voice. "May I call you that? I want you to know that I spotted your dress all the way across this room and I made Emilio bring me over. It's absolutely *adorable.*"

"I think so, too," Frank Fisher said, "but I'm sure it would be worth my life to say so first."

We all laughed.

"But what really impressed us," Fisher went on, "is how you all picked up so smoothly when the singer got cold feet. That was pretty remarkable, we thought, didn't we, El?"

Ellie Fisher nodded several times. "We certainly did," she said.

"It occurred to me to wonder just how you people are able to handle a situation like that. It must be that you know the music well, you can't be that fast on your feet, am I right?"

I was about to respond when I realized that he wasn't listening for an answer. The Frank Fishers of this world have all the answers they need, and they don't want any more. So I nodded the way his wife did, and said something meaningless about hard practice and clean living.

"Well, I'll tell you one thing," Fisher declared. "I wish more individuals in industry had the discipline and dedication of you folks in music. Then you'd really see something."

"Oh, yes, of course," I said.

Fisher was about to elaborate when a voice behind me cut in. "Please forgive me, I must— Ah, Emilio! I must leave, but not before I thank you for so entertaining an evening."

It was Reyes Garcia y Lopez, immaculate in evening dress, wearing a smile and looking as amiable as a barracuda can look.

Count Emilio was standing right next to me, and to my surprise I felt him go almost rigid with alarm. "The pleasure is entirely mine," he said in a forced voice. And then he did a completely unnatural thing. He became rude. "No doubt you remember these musicians," he said, indicating us with a jerk of his head.

"But of course," said Garcia evenly, nodding to us.

Another jerk of the head. "Mr. and Mrs. Fisher. *Stranieri*, from America."

Frank Fisher blinked at the sudden chill in the atmosphere, and Ellie Fisher looked flustered, but they smiled politely and said that they were delighted.

Garcia responded in kind.

Midway through the bowing and hand-kissing, the count suddenly seized Garcia's sleeve. "Reyes," he said. "Over there is someone I definitely want you to meet. Come with me. Now, at once!" And he actually began to pull at Garcia's arm.

Garcia looked embarrassed. "Emilio, please . . . ," he said, trying to free himself. But another voice interrupted the tug-of-war.

"Papa!" It was the very young, very pretty girl in beige who had been with him at the concert.

As she came up to us, we could see that her face was excited and her eyes were sparkling, and it was hard to keep from smiling at her enthusiasm. She was not alone. In tow behind her, the pleased look on his face giving way to total consternation, was none other than Terry Monza.

The girl began in Spanish. *"Papa, por favor—"*

"Doucement, doucement, mon ange," said Garcia. The warmth in

his voice astounded me. "First, greet Monsieur French and Mademoiselle Craine, who played for us tonight, and Monsieur and Madame Fisher. The count, of course, you know. *Mes amis*, this is my daughter, Marie-Eve."

Marie-Eve dropped us a curtsey that must have come straight out of the convent. I felt mortified to have mistaken this bubbly teenager for Garcia's mistress.

"And now, what is it, sweetheart?"

"Papa—"

"And remember to speak English." Garcia turned to me. "I always ask her to speak English when we are with Americans. It is so good for her accent."

"Please, Papa, Terry has asked me—excuse me, this is Terry Monza, Terry, this is my father—if we can go out with some of the people in the . . . in the opera. After the party. Only for coffee, Papa. Then he will bring me straight home."

Garcia kept his face politely inscrutable, but I could see the confusion in his eyes. I knew how he felt. If ever a situation was worthy of the hometown of the Capulets and the Montagues, it had to be this one.

Finally, he looked at his watch and shook his head. "It's already late, my dear. I'm afraid the answer must be no."

"Oh, but, Father . . ." Her face fell, but there was no sullenness in her reaction, only disappointment. She really was a delicious child.

Garcia looked around for help, but none of us would meet his eye.

Finally, like every other father of a pretty daughter, he gave in. "There will be others with you?" he asked her.

"Yes, of course."

"And you will not be too late?"

"No way, sir," said Terry. "We're all tired from playing."

"Very well, then," Garcia said. "But be home by *medianoche*. Or I will send the airplanes after you." I knew he meant the *carabinieri*: their broad-brimmed triangular hats had earned them the nickname.

Marie-Eve looked ecstatic. She thanked her father, curtseyed

again and whisked Terry away as if she were afraid Garcia
might change his mind.

Over his shoulder, Terry himself cast us a glance that mingled
delight and despair.

Frank Fisher cleared his throat. "Now, that's what I call a
charmer! She certainly does you credit, Signor Garcia."

Garcia smiled sourly. "She is a good child, and I am very fond
of her, but she persuades me too easily. I am not sure"—he
looked straight at me—"that I did not make a serious mistake."

"We all make mistakes," I said.

"That is true," Garcia said. "And some we regret more than
others." It could have been a backhand apology for the incident
at the Ortofrutticolo or a threat to do worse next time. Or it
could have meant nothing at all.

Frank Fisher looked from one of us to the other, uncom-
prehending. For Frank Fisher, there were no mistakes to regret.

"And now, you really must forgive me," Garcia said. "For me,
if not for my daughter, it is time to go to bed."

"Must you leave us?" The count spoke courteously: the little
contretemps about Marie-Eve's night life seemed to have restored his good humor. But I noticed that he made no effort to
detain Garcia or to introduce him to that other guest he'd been
so insistent about a few moments before.

"Emilio, I must." Garcia congratulated the count, bowed over
Ellie Fisher's hand, nodded civilly to Jackie and me and headed
for the door.

The count sighed with relief, as though some sort of crisis
were over.

"What a fascinating man!" Ellie Fisher said in her calm voice.
"Is he an old friend, Emilio?"

"Say rather an old acquaintance," the count replied. "From
the war."

Both Fishers were silent. They were sophisticated enough not
to ask too many questions when the count spoke in that tone of
voice about the war.

Then Ellie Fisher said brightly: "Jackie, can I ask you something? How ever do you manage to carry that great big cello

from place to place? I mean, without getting those awful bulgy muscles in your upper arms?"

In our business, you get used to questions like that one.

"It's not a cello, it's a viola da gamba," said Jackie and explained that it wasn't weight but bulk and frailty that made the gamba hard to lug around.

Then Frank Fisher wanted to know how much public support the Antiqua Players received. My answer, one five-hundred-dollar grant from New York State Council on the Arts, somewhat undercut his argument that while he was all for the arts, damned if he could see how the economy could afford all those millions of taxpayer dollars worth of subsidies to hippie artists.

That's when the count decided to take the Fishers away for a look at his Modiglianis.

"You shouldn't have said it," Jackie said reprovingly when they'd gone.

"Said what?"

"You know perfectly well what."

"All I said was, I thought it was wasteful to spend money on art when what the U.S. really needed was a bigger defense budget and more atomic weapons. I was *agreeing* with him, for God's sake."

"You were being sarcastic, and you know it. You always do that to people, even when they mean well."

"I was just being polite. Anyway," I yawned, "I'm too tired to fight over Frank Fisher."

"Me, too. How about one more glass of wine?"

We were just finishing our nightcaps when we spotted the count hurrying toward us through the thinning crowd. "Something's happened," Jackie said.

"And it ain't good," I said.

"Please come with me," the count said urgently. "We must talk."

He led us by a back corridor to his office and served us coffee with his own hands, pouring the rich black liquid shakily into the cups of translucent Ginori porcelain.

"What's wrong?" Jackie asked him.

The count made one final effort. "Nothing is *wrong*, " he said.
"Come off it," I said.
"Very well. I have just had word from the representative of the Americans."
"And?"
"They want their wine delivered at once. Can we do it?"
"How soon is at once?" I asked him.
"Within seventy-two hours."
"I don't know," I said.
"You must," the count said. "You must, or . . ." The look on his face told me more about the alternative than I wanted to know.
"I have to make a few phone calls," I said.
"Yes, of course," said count. "Go right away."
"Wait a minute," Jackie said as we rose. "You were with Mr. and Mrs. Fisher, weren't you? When did you have time—"
"Jackie," I said, "don't be dense."
"Yes," said the count. "Frank Fisher is the man in charge of the deal with the Americans."

Take into account the appointed area in which you are about to dance, being master in the art of using space.

Cornazano,
Art of Dancing

CHAPTER FIFTEEN

In the end, all five of us took the bus to Yugoslavia.

We had no problem at all with Vivi and Petar. Even at 6 A.M., which is when I reached them at the Giusti, they were bright-eyed and ready to deal. "No problem, man," Petar said when I told him we needed immediate delivery. "You come tomorrow, today even, we'll load you right up."

"How about money?"

"No problem," he said again. "You fix up a letter of credit, see? Your bank to our bank. We load, you get the shipping papers, we cash your letter, you take off. And, hey . . . we'll give you a good discount for dollars."

It took an hour with the count and some more phoning to agree on price. The final price was a complicated mixture of lire and dollars. Petar and the count seemed to understand it perfectly, but my head was aching long before we were through.

Then there was the little matter of credit. To this day, I'm not sure whether Count Emilio lent us eight hundred thousand dollars or we lent him eight hundred thousand dollars, but the net result was an account in Terry's and my names with eight hundred thousand dollars in it that we couldn't touch.

The final hassle was over licensing. We didn't want the count to know where the wine was coming from, so we had to take care of this on our own. There was no way to do it over the phone, so Terry, Petar, Vivi and I trooped down together to the provincial offices. They were housed in a vast nineteenth-century marble palazzo right across from police headquarters. I was scared stiff lest Commissario Ratner spot me, grab me and start asking embarrassing questions.

That didn't happen, but what did happen was almost as un-
nerving.

At the office of agriculture, we soon found out that: (a) the
Italians, being wine exporters, were less than eager to let anybody *import* wine from somewhere else; and (b) the official in
charge was highly inclined to refer the entire matter to his superiors in Milan. These gentlemen were not available at present,
signori, and, alas! were not expected to be available for many
days. You know how it is . . .

Petar did indeed know how it was, and he and Vivi knew
exactly what to do about it.

"You mean," the official said when they paused to catch their
breath, "this wine is not to be resold here in Italy?"

"No, Signor Commendatore. It will be exported and will earn
foreign exchange for a fine Italian firm, one located right here in
Verona."

"In that case . . ." The man scratched his eyebrow absently
with the end of his ballpoint pen. I wondered later whether he'd
known or guessed something, but if he had it was to our benefit.
He bent busily over his forms and rubber stamps and, a minute
later, handed us our permit and wished us good luck with our
transaction.

"You see?" said Petar. "I told you it would be easy. We're
going to take off, and we'll see you later in Bled."

"Why not go together?" I asked.

Petar laughed. "You ever ride in the back of a Zastava?

"Oh."

"Besides, it's better if two go out and two come back," Vivi
said.

We walked them to their car, and they were right. From Verona to Bled is only about 220 miles, but I'd hate to have to do
those miles in the rear seat of their little red subsubcompact.

Vivi tied her hair back with a scarf and got behind the wheel.

"Don't be late," she said. "We're going to cook you a great
supper and then throw a party."

"Drive carefully," said Petar.

"Yes, drive carefully," Vivi echoed. "Maybe you shouldn't

drive at all." She took her hands off the wheel and waggled them
to signify narrow, winding roads.

"That's a good idea," Petar said. "Take the bus. There's one
every hour. Change in Ljubljana."

"You won't be so tired for the party!" Vivi said as they pulled
away.

It was ten-thirty when we got back to the Palazzo Sabinetti
and went into conference with the others.

"You are not going anywhere," Jackie said. "You are certainly
not going to Yugoslavia."

"But—"

"Not without me."

"But—"

"In fact, not without Ralph and David, either."

"Jackie, listen," I said. "It doesn't take all five of us to fix up
this wine thing."

"That's true," Ralph said, "but it's beautiful country and I
want to go."

"I'm with Ralph," David said. "Let's see some sights."

I looked at Terry.

"Sure," he said, "why not?"

So we grabbed our passports and left word with Orlando on
our way out that we'd be away sight-seeing for the night. We
walked to American Express and cashed some travelers' checks,
and then Jackie remembered that in the mountains, where Bled
is, it's cold in June. So back we went to the palazzo to collect
warm clothing, and finally, just before noon, we started across
the Ponte Nuovo. No thugs accosted us, no policemen blew the
whistle. Fifteen minutes later, the big black-windowed Trieste
bus nosed its way past the Giusti Gardens and down the Via
San Nazzaro in search of the A4, with the Antiqua Players
safely on board.

The safe, conservative way to go from Verona to Bled is to
cross the Yugoslav frontier at Trieste, take main roads to Ljubljana and transfer there.

Thanks to Terry, we didn't go that way. "It's a lot quicker to
get off at Gorizia and grab the local bus." Jackie looked dubious,

but on the map a fat red line indicating a major road led from Gorizia to Bled, and it was only thirty-six miles.

So we scrambled off the Trieste bus at Gorizia, had our passports stamped at the frontier and scrambled onto a small but very high-tech-looking bus that Terry said was bound for Bled. A lot of other people got on the bus, too. We struck up a lively conversation, in broken English and gesticulation, with the members of an Alpine hiking club on their way to a holiday in the mountains.

The driver climbed aboard, the automatic door shut with a hiss and we were off for Bled. Or rather, we would have been off for Bled if the bus had started. But the bus didn't start. After a few battery-draining tries, the driver levered himself from his seat and disappeared: groans from the passengers, banging noises from the rear and an overwhelming smell of diesel fuel soon told us where he'd gone.

A moment later, the driver came back aboard, accompanied by a disillusioned man in shirt-sleeves, tie and clipboard.

The disillusioned man made a brief announcement in several languages, none of them English.

After more groans, everybody else arose, gathered up their carry-ons, and filed out. Hearts heavy, we followed suit.

The driver led us across a parking lot to our new bus.

Instead of sleek aerodynamic lines, this vehicle presented a rather squared-off profile. Its motor was in the front, under a blunt hood. A big spare tire decorated its rear. Its seats were uncushioned, vinyl-covered benches.

"Hey, whoa!" said David, "I used to ride this bus on the way to P.S. 34. I'll bet I could find my initials in here somewhere."

"Never mind the nostalgia," I said. "Let's just hope it starts."

It did start, and once started it kept going at a bone-rattling, conversation-deadening seventeen miles per hour (estimated).

We were about two miles outside Gorizia when the driver rounded a curve to the left, slowed sharply and, with a horrible grinding of gears, turned straight up the side of a mountain.

Somebody's satchel, insecurely moored, slid all the way down the center aisle and fetched up under the rearmost bench.

"Oh, dear God," someone moaned. It was me.

The odd thing was that none of the others on board said or did anything about this hair-raising maneuver. The elderly woman on my right kept on with her knitting. The Alpinists up front continued to argue about something: schnapps versus slivovitz, maybe. Terry was sound asleep. I couldn't see Ralph and David, but they certainly weren't sounding off as if they were agitated. Even Jackie, a child of the prairie who studiously avoids heights, sat calmly in her seat, her nose in a paperback thriller.

"Jackie," I whispered hoarsely.

"Hm-m?"

"Look out the window."

Obediently, she looked. "What is it? I can't see a thing."

She was right. A thick fog, obviously a high-altitude cumulonimbus, blanketed the view.

"We're going . . . up," I said.

"Well, of course. Bled is in the mountains."

Just then, the bus leveled off briefly. Then it gave a lurch, gathered speed and, with a merry quack of its horn, began to careen headlong down the other side of the mountain.

Whenever I could bring myself to open my eyes, I caught glimpses of the magnificent scenery that went speeding by. You know the sort of thing: vertical drops of fifty thousand feet or more straight into the boulder-strewn gorges of roaring torrents; farmhouses perched like sparrows on the edges of precipices; sloping meadows dotted with flowers too dumb to grow in nice safe valleys; once in a while a whole little village, complete with church, built teetering on a hillside.

"It's gorgeous, I must admit," I said to Jackie. "But aren't you scared?"

To dodge the tractor that came chugging stolidly toward us, dead on the crown of the road, our driver swerved the bus so that its right front wheel, I swear, was over the edge of an unfenced eighty-foot drop. I cowered back in my seat. The lady with the knitting gave me a strange look and shook her head.

"I *am* scared," Jackie said. "Quiller has followed these people into the jungle and the only way out is to get aboard their air-plane, and—"

"What on earth are you talking about?"

"My book," said Jackie. "Haven't you got anything to read?"

"The hell with it," I said. "Here we are about to be killed or maimed and all you want to do is curl up with a thriller."

Jackie gave me an impudent look. "I can't curl up with *you,* can I? Not here."

"No, but you can hold my hand while you read, so that when we plunge to our doom I will die happy."

"Okay, but how will I turn pages?"

It was a knotty problem, but we managed all the way to Bled.

I was thrilled to see Bled and would have loved to see more of it. From the bus, I was treated to a look at a huge, shimmering lake. Its shoreline was dominated by old-fashioned resort hotels of the kind in which trios play Offenbach and Grétry at teatime. Best of all, several of Bled's streets were horizontal. But a tour of the beautiful old town was not to be. As we descended in the central square, we were greeted by furious honking and arm-waving from a big van parked in the no-parking zone in front of the prefecture.

"How come you came on this thing, man?" Petar asked. "We thought you'd be coming on the big bus."

"Don't mind him," Vivi said. "He was afraid you weren't coming, that something had gone wrong, but I knew you were. And who are *you?*" She gave David a dazzling smile.

We introduced everybody to everybody and clambered into the van. Petar drove and Vivi talked. "How did you like the trip up from Podbrdo? Were you scared? I love your sweater, Jackie. Did they name you after Jackie O.? Have you arranged the fi-nancing? You should see the woolens they weave in Bled. En-glish woolens—poof! What bank are you using? Isn't Slovenia the most beautiful country? Do you have sheep in the United States of America?"

This went on for about ten minutes, with Petar saying at intervals, "Shut *up,* Vivi," and driving us deeper and deeper into the countryside. Finally, he made a sharp left turn off the paved road and drove the van into a narrow passageway, almost a tunnel, between two wings of a massive stone farmhouse.

Chickens scurried away as we braked to a halt in a gravel-surfaced courtyard, but a great black-and-white rooster with a huge feathery crest eyed us contemptuously before stalking away on hairy legs.

"Oh," cried Jackie, "he's *beautiful!* What is he, Vivi? A Houdan?"

"You know poultry?" Vivi asked incredulously.

"I guess so. I looked after ours for years."

"But that's wonderful! That is Laszlo. He's a Polish—"

"Too much!" Petar said. "Listen, while these two chicken farmers go at it, why don't we go inside and get on with the paper work?"

Ralph and David excused themselves to wander around the farmstead, so Terry and I followed Petar across the courtyard and through a big wooden door into the main building.

The offices were a revelation. They were as up to date as the exterior of the building was rustic, with indirect lighting, modern furnishings, a Telex and even Cyrillic-alphabet Selectrics.

Through a plate-glass window, I could see across a broad valley. Staked vines ran in neat rows straight across the whole width of the valley and up the slope of a green hillside, a mile or more away. Farther up, the hill was terraced for still more vines. The vines must have numbered in the millions.

In the foreground was a long two-story shed. Alongside, a convoy of eight enormous double-bodied tanker trucks was lined up. A couple of the drivers were seated on the running board of the first truck in line.

"Some people would call it their *cave.* But what it is is our tank farm," Petar said proudly. "Your wine's in there now."

"And the trucks?"

"Waiting to load your wine."

I handed Petar the letter of credit on the count's bank. He read it carefully. "Excuse me," he said. "I want our *Finanzdirektor* to see this."

He rose and left the office, returning a moment later with a ruddy-faced man in an electric-blue suit. "Gentlemen, this is Anton."

Anton nodded, fixed steel-rimmed granny glasses on his nose and slowly and carefully perused the letter of credit. He nodded again, smiled and handed the letter back to Petar.

"Everything's okey-dokey," said Petar cheerfully. "You got the money, honey, we got the wine. Now let's *us* get the money and *you* get the wine. Come on."

He walked us downstairs and out the door, a different door from the one through which we'd entered. This one led out to the loading area by the tank farm. The air was filled with the sour, slightly acid odor of spilled wine.

One of the tanker drivers came up to us. Petar exchanged a few words with him, I guess in Slovenian, and the driver stumped away to talk with his mates.

Petar turned back to us. "First, you take a little drink," he said. "So you know that what you're getting is what you ordered."

"And don't tell him not to bother," Terry muttered to me so Petar couldn't overhear. "We're supposed to be wine experts, so make like you are one."

We went into the dimly lit shed and stopped at the nearest of the long row of stainless steel tanks. The thin glass pipe gauge running up its side was filled with wine.

Petar wasted no time on ceremony. He simply handed us each a waterglass-sized tumbler—mine had stylized tulips on it, like a Kraft cheese spread container back home—turned a spigot, filled a plain glass jug a third full and poured us each a generous sample from the jug.

Terry took a sip and sucked in air noisily, then swished the wine around in his mouth for several seconds. I watched him covertly and followed suit. I thought the wine tasted good, only maybe a little perfumy.

Terry, however, made a sour face. "You sure this isn't a Traminer?"

"No!" Petar said emphatically. "A Riesling from near here,

some Smederevka. Give it air, the *Würzigheit* goes away." He shook the jug to agitate the wine.

"Leave the wine alone," Terry said sharply. Then: "Got any bread?"

"I have bread," Petar said, producing a loaf and cutting us each a chunk. Even I knew that the bread would take away the wine taste.

After a minute or two, Terry sampled the wine again. "Still tastes fruity to me," he said. "What do you think?" As he spoke, he winked at me surreptitiously.

"It gets sharper," I said.

"Hey, man, really—" Petar began to protest.

Terry silenced him with a glance. "Just take it easy, huh?" We've got a lot of dough at stake in this deal."

He took another bite of bread and went through a whole ritual of masticating it thoroughly. Then he made Petar wait a good five minutes before he tried the wine a third time.

"I *think* it's okay," he said finally. "I *think* so."

"I agree," I said. I just wanted to get going. "Let's let them load up."

"That's good, man," said Petar fervently. "We brought a lot of wine in here for you, so that's good. You want to test the other tanks?"

Dutifully, we ate our bread, tasted samples from three more tanks and approved all three. Then we went outside, and events began to move quickly. Hoses were brought in from the steam room where they were kept sterilized and hooked up to the tankers. We had to check each gauge on each tanker for a zero reading, initial a score sheet to that effect and watch while each gauge was sealed. Then the pumps were turned on and the wine began to flow.

"That's it, man," Petar said. "There's nothing more to do until about seven o'clock. Unless you guys want to stand around here and make sure we're not siphoning off any wine or sneaking any water into the load."

"Does that happen?" I asked.

"Sometimes, but not this time. I give you my word."

The strange thing was, I believed him.

"Come on," Petar said. "We'll find the women and take off for a real drink and dinner. Then we'll rest up. By then the loading will be finished and we can close the sale. Which one of you is going?"

"Going where?" I asked.

"With the trucks."

Terry and I looked at each other.

"I guess that's me," Terry said.

The Italians . . . frame ditties to [their Galliardes],
which in their *mascaradoes* they sing and daunce . . .
Thomas Morley,
*Plaine and Easie Introduction to
Practicall Musicke* (1597)

CHAPTER SIXTEEN

Ralph was driving when they stopped us.

Vivi had promised to cook for us, but Petar had swept aside the promise and taken us to "my special hangout," an open-air café where the food was good and the wine and music beguiling. There, he'd talked such nonsense to Jackie that even Vivi blushed with embarrassment. Naturally, we'd missed the last bus for Ljubljana.

"I'll drive you, man," Petar said, "but we've got to get those trucks on the road. You better try Kompas."

Kompas produced a Fiat 128 that we could actually drop off in Verona. And so, at about ten o'clock, we waved goodbye to Vivi, Petar and Terry and set off. It was drizzling and misty, and Ralph wanted no part of the road to Gorizia. But the traffic was light on the Ljubljana highway and the Ljubljana–Trieste *avtocesta* was almost empty. Before midnight, we were back in Italy.

They must have been watching for us at Palmanova, where the lights were bright enough to identify us when Ralph slowed to negotiate the lane change. But they wanted to be sure, because they followed us virtually the entire length of the E7 before pulling us over onto the shoulder a few hundred meters short of the exit at Soave. We never saw them until their headlights began to blink and their blue dome flasher started up.

"Damn," Ralph muttered between his teeth as he tapped the brake to slow the 128. "I've been under sixty the whole way."

Jackie, David and I were too drowsy to be suspicious. Even when the tough-looking youth in leather jacket and shiny boots ignored Ralph's proffered license and said curtly: *"Seguimi,"* we still thought we'd been nailed for speeding.

The youth stamped back to his cruiser. His partner swung it back onto the pavement and swerved down the Soave exit ramp with us in his wake.

It was very dark away from the highway, and the air was damp. A rich earth smell rose from the tilled soil on either side of the secondary road. I began to feel uneasy.

Up ahead, brake lights flashed and the cruiser's indicator told us it was turning right.

The turn took us into a narrow lane between two fields.

"Funny place for a police station," Ralph said.

"Yeah," said David. "Maybe we should turn around and get the hell out of here."

"Good idea," I said. "Think the other cop will let us by?"

"What other cop?" Jackie asked.

"The one hiding back there in the olive grove."

The asphalt gave way to fine gravel. The road grew narrower and sank between stony banks on either side. Topping the banks, silhouetted like lances against the starry sky, were regiments of tall poles carrying grapevines. The atmosphere was palpably, melodramatically oppressive.

"Christus!" Jackie said shakily. "If a rabbit ran in front of us, I think I'd scream my head off."

Ralph put on the brakes as the car ahead came to a stop.

For a long moment, we sat there in the darkness. Then light from a powerful electric lantern flooded the scene and we could see that both cars were parked in the dooryard of a modern cement-and-stucco villa. Its shutters were closed, but lights were on inside.

Quickly, Ralph backed the 128 around to face the way we'd come in.

The lantern bobbled as the tough kid in boots ran toward us, shouting in Italian. Three or four other men materialized out of the shadows and closed in on our car.

"I think they want us to stop," Jackie said.

Ralph switched off his lights and cut the engine.

The kid shone the lantern in our faces, blinding us.

"Cops, my ass," said David. "We're being kidnapped."

"What the hell do you think you're doing?" I yelled at the kid outside. My heart was pounding a mile a minute.

He yelled back something incomprehensible.

"You come get us!" David shouted.

There was silence. Then the little bastard dimmed the lantern and rapped on Ralph's window with something metallic.

"Oh, Christ," I said.

It was a gun, and it looked as big as a cannon.

Reluctantly, we got out of the car.

"*Seguimi!*" the kid said again, gesturing with his gun. He swaggered in front of us toward the doorway to the villa, then waited for us and motioned us inside.

We stood blinking in the brightly lit entrance hall. A door opened and a neatly dressed figure emerged.

"Surprise, surprise," Ralph said.

"Come in, please," said Reyes Garcia y Lopez.

The room we entered, comfortably furnished in overstuffed modern, with bland abstract paintings on the off-white walls, was a good room in which to play urbane villain. It had ample room for pacing, a mirrored bar from which sinister cocktails could be dispensed, even a radio that could be turned up to mask the yells of victims.

To his credit, Garcia refused the part. He didn't stride back and forth, rub his hands or gloat. He didn't offer us so much as a ginger ale. As soon as we were seated, he rasped out his number one question.

"Mr. French, why are you stealing wine from Count Emilio?"

If he'd meant to bowl me over, he'd scored a strike. "Why are we *what?*"

"Please, Mr. French. It is late and we are all fatigued. I know that you have obtained samples of Sabinetti vintages. I know that you are in contact with foreign buyers of wine. I know that at this moment a tanker group is en route from Trieste under your orders. I know all of these things. But most of all, I know that the count does not know, because I asked him not two hours ago."

Hearing Garcia's words, I began to sweat. I felt as if I'd arrived at Carnegie Hall to play quartets and found I'd forgotten my fiddle. The situation would be comical, no doubt, if it weren't so deadly. It wouldn't be easy to persuade the hard-eyed operator who'd had us brought here that he'd gotten things upside down. The young oaf lounging on the sofa and resting his boots on a marble coffee table would probably be thrilled to be told to start beating the truth out of one of us, though if he picked the wrong one he might be in for a surprise.

But the biggest problem staring me in the face was that our friend Count Emilio wasn't letting his friend Garcia in on the truth about us. I knew this was important, but there just wasn't enough time to sit there and figure out why.

Garcia was eyeing me expectantly, waiting for an answer. So were Jackie, Ralph and David. The lad in boots was the only incurious person in the room. He was busy cleaning his nails with the tip of the blade of a large switchblade knife.

"Those tanker trucks aren't empty." My voice sounded hollow and unconvincing and not like my own. My answer sounded equally hollow, but I couldn't think of anything else to say.

"No?" Garcia's expression didn't change, but something told me that I'd handed him a little surprise.

"My associate Mr. Monza knows a lot about wine. We are *buying* wine. The count is storing it for us until we can resell it." Technically, what I'd said was absolutely true, even though the resale wasn't the innocent transaction I wanted Garcia to think it was.

He *was* thinking, I saw with relief. His left hand had come up to fondle his upper lip in a gesture that suggested he had once had a moustache to stroke. He continued to stare at me, but his eyes looked a fraction less hostile. "And the samples, Mr. French?"

"You're misinformed," I said. "Those were not samples of the count's wine but of wine we were thinking of buying."

"Yes," Garcia said thoughtfully, after a pause. "You *would* say that. But it would be simple to prove your point . . . Mr. French, where are the samples now? In your auto?" I was paralyzed. The samples were in Bled. But to tell this to Garcia would be to tell him that we were buying wine in Yugoslavia. I really didn't want him to start asking me seriously why we were shipping Yugoslav wine to Verona.

David, languid as always, saved the day. "We drank the samples," he announced.

This time, Garcia really was astonished. "You *drank* the sample bottles?"

"They weren't cool enough," David said, "but we didn't need them anymore and we were thirsty. We tossed the bottles out the window somewhere."

Garcia stood and gazed at us. He massaged his upper lip some more. Then, without a word, he left the room. This seemed to be some sort of signal to the kid who was guarding us. He put away his switchblade, got to his feet and came over to us, walking stiff-legged in his shiny leather boots. He looked both silly and dangerous.

First, the kid said something in Italian to Jackie. His meaning was unmistakable. Jackie flushed and looked at me. I gave her a slight shrug. Be patient, I was saying to her, with a thug like this you can put up with a few insults.

With a sneer and another phrase, the kid turned to Ralph.

"The same to you, my dear," Ralph said, showing his teeth in a smile.

"Take it easy, baby," David said to Ralph.

The kid moved closer and swung his arm as if he were going to backhand Ralph across the face. Still smiling, Ralph watched him without moving a muscle.

"Ralph . . . ," said Jackie.

Just then, Garcia came back into the room.

The youth sneered again. But he turned away and resumed his seat and his nail-cleaning. Garcia might have been making a routine phone call. But my guess was that leaving us alone with the teenage menace had been meant to soften us up.

Now it was Garcia's turn. "Mr. French, there are things about you and your people I do not understand."

"We aren't in the least mysterious," I said.

Garcia went on as if he hadn't heard me. "A few days ago, I begged you to spare the count's feelings, as he had recently suffered a personal tragedy."

"I remember," I said. "In what way have we disturbed the count?"

Again Garcia ignored my question. "I was being polite," he said. "I was suggesting politely that what you were doing was disturbing to me."

I said nothing.

"You now know," he went on, "that I have the power to do certain things that most people cannot do."

"Yes," I said again. "Like contacting your important friends in transportation firms and government bureaus to find out who is arranging shipping."

"I can do that," Garcia said.

"And persuading the *stradali* to look the other way while you trap innocent people on the highway. They probably think you are a big shot from the CIA."

"Perhaps I am," Garcia said.

"Perhaps you are," I said, "although I doubt it. Because your friends in these places are feeding you false reports. We are not stealing the count's wine. We are buying wine. As for your friends in the police, you have probably told Commissario Ratner that you had some way to get information from us. But there's nothing to get, and that's embarrassing, isn't it?"

If it was, Garcia's face wasn't admitting it.

"The commissario has a murder to solve," I reminded him. "He thinks we can help him solve it."

"I had no part in Caspardino's death," Garcia said quickly. Too quickly? Maybe.

"I am happy to hear it. But if anything happens to us, or if I fail to report to the commissario on schedule, he will come looking for us. And if he finds out that you are responsible, he will come looking for *you*. I know the commissario is your friend. But even if he is your brother, I do not think he will allow you to keep us here indefinitely. The risk would be too great.

"We are tired and we have rehearsals and a concert tomorrow. The wisest thing would be for you to let us go back to Verona."

A long moment went by.

Then Garcia said: "Mr. French, if you had some way to prove your story that you are buying wine for your own account—"

"Oh, for God's sake," I said wearily. "Go call up your friends at the bank. They'll tell you that we opened a credit account. Why would we need a credit account if we were *stealing* the count's wine?"

Another lengthy silence.

"What is the name of your bank?"

"Why should I tell you?"

Garcia sighed. "To save time, Mr. French."

"Count Emilio told me the other day that you are helping him," I said. "I only hope it's true."

Garcia made a movement with his lips that could have been interpreted as a smile. Oh, well. To get us out of here in one piece had to cost something.

"Banco di Trieste ed Adriatico," I said, "the Venice branch."

"You understand what a mistake it would be to mislead me on this matter," said Garcia.

My turn to smile.

"Marco!" Thug-in-Boots got up and put away his knife.

"Escort Mr. French and his friends to their car and direct them to Verona."

"*Sì, signore!*"

To get to the door, Marco did have to cross the room. He didn't have to swerve to pass close to Ralph, who had just risen to his feet. He didn't have to purse his lips in a contemptuous smirk. He didn't have to reach out a contemptuous hand toward Ralph's shoulder.

Jackie cried out in warning, but she was too late.

Poor Marco.

Marco's booted feet pinwheeled forward and upward in slow motion. His head flipped backward and down and finally came to rest—almost gently, it seemed—on the marble floor.

As it hit, loose change spilled from his pocket. One coin spun on its edge for a split second, then rolled under a chair. The little rattling noise it made was the only sound in the room until the rest of Marco landed. Marco's gun bulged out of his waistband. Why it didn't go off, I'll never know.

Ralph let go of Marco's left wrist. Marco's arm flopped to the floor.

"*Ay, hombre!*" Garcia said quietly. He sounded impressed. None of us uttered a word. We knew all about Ralph's martial arts trophies. Now Marco and Garcia knew, too.

Ralph brushed the hair back from his forehead. "Well!" he said brightly. "Shall we go?"

Garcia simply looked at us, then at Marco, who was beginning to moan a little and move around. He stood back to let us get to the door.

We went outside to the 128. The "cruiser" that had pulled us over was gone. Nobody seemed to be watching.

"You drive," Ralph said, handing me the keys. "It's been a long day."

"Cut out the Gary Cooper act," I said. "You were fantastic and you know it."

"That *awful* creep. I mean, I just couldn't."

"Everybody else okay?" I asked.

For a moment, Jackie clung to me in the dark. Then she said: "Wait till you see what *I* do to Marco's brother."

We all laughed, but shakily, and got ourselves into the car. My own legs were so rubbery that I could barely make the pedals work, but I got the 128 started and drove slowly back up the lane.

"I never thought I'd be *glad* to see a superhighway," said David as we drove up the westbound entrance ramp.

"Yes, and you know what this one is called?" Ralph said.

"No idea," I said.

"The Serenissima. Don't you love it?"

For now, it was serene enough. Only market trucks and the sun rising slowly at our back kept us company into Verona.

When a dancer's companions perceive that
he is weary they go and steal his damsel
and dance with her themselves.

Arbeau,
Orchesographie

CHAPTER SEVENTEEN

Sometimes you play better without sleep. Don't ask me why. Or
rather, do ask me, and I'll give you my current pet theory. My
theory is that fatigue loosens the muscles and, at the same time,
dulls the forebrain. This gives the subconscious its chance to
take over. The subconscious remembers everything—every
tricky fingering, every subtle bowing, every nuance of phrase—
and your relaxed muscles, freed of the intellectual tyranny of
the forebrain, execute everything perfectly. That's what I think.
I once asked a Columbia University experimental psychologist
about it. He looked at me with pity, scratched his shiny pate and
mumbled something about dextrose and lactic acid before turning away to talk to a squat young woman who played French
horn.

At ten o'clock the next morning, we regrouped in room three,
the rehearsal room with the beautiful fireplace. It was a Sunday.
We knew this because of the church bells. Their banging had
fatally disturbed our brief snatches of slumber. The Sunday
bells had accompanied us as we primed ourselves with espresso
at breakfast. Like jealous competitors, they were doing their
best to sabotage our dress rehearsal. But they weren't suc-
ceeding.

"Can Terry really play Herkimer that fast?" "Herkimer" was
our code name for *Le Forze d'Hercole*, a sixteenth-century hit tune
we were playing on krummhorn and gamba.

"Sure," Jackie said, "why not?"

"No reason," I said, "if you think you can cut it. It'll set up
the Frescobaldi nicely."

"Be stately, Ralph," said Jackie.

Ralph gave us the opening bars of the *La Folia* variations.

"More stately," I said. "More fretwork."

He rolled out the opening again, this time with elaborate ornamentation in both hands.

"Much better. Quite nice, in fact."

"Well . . . It's the first thing I'm playing. I don't know if I'll be warmed up enough."

"You're playing in the opening number," I said.

"Oh, don't be *difficult*," Ralph said.

"Give it a shot," I said.

"I'll try."

"Now, where's What's-her-name?" I said. "I want to go over the *Quel Sguardo*. Sabrina! Where the hell are you?"

We were so used to Sabrina's showing up late that we hadn't given her absence a thought. But she'd never been this late before.

"I'll run up to her room and wake her," Jackie said.

She was gone only a few minutes.

"It's funny," she said when she came back into the room. "I banged really hard on her door and there was no answer. And I asked Orlando and he said he hadn't seen her since yesterday morning."

"That *is* funny," I agreed.

"Maybe she met somebody at the *Arianna* party," David said.

"No," said Jackie. "Orlando definitely said he'd seen her yesterday. She asked him to get her extra copies of the paper, for the reviews."

"My God, the reviews!" I said, aghast. I'd absolutely forgotten that there were such things, which will give you a rough idea of the state of my mind. "How were they?"

"I was wondering when you'd wake up," Ralph said complacently. "If you hadn't been so busy stuffing yourself with rolls and marmalade, you would have seen for yourself at breakfast."

"We did fine," Jackie said, producing a wad of newspapers.

I glanced at the columns of Italian print, registering enough of the phraseology to see that it was mostly favorable. "Sounds okay. But what about Sabrina?"

"I can answer your question, Mr. French. She is quite safe— so far." Count Emilio paused in the doorway to deliver this bombshell. Then he came all the way into the room. The count was freshly barbered and, as always, beautifully turned out. He looked ghastly.

"What do you mean?" I demanded. "Where is she?"

"She is with the Fishers. You remember . . ."

Ellie and Frank, from Montclair. And the mob. "Sure I remember. But why?"

"They are at their villa in the hills. Beyond my winery. They are waiting to see if the wine is shipped. If it is shipped today, they will bring her back. So far, they are treating her as their guest."

"They better bring her back," David said. "We've got a concert tonight."

The count stared at him. "If the winery's warehouse receipt is not signed by four o'clock," he said, "they will keep her. They will . . . hurt her."

"Oh, no!" Jackie exclaimed.

"They mean what they say," the count added quietly, and I believed him.

"Okay," I said. "Call the Fishers. Have them meet us at the winery at three o'clock. With Sabrina. We'll give them their wine then. Will your people work on a Sunday?"

"They will have to," said the count. He went off to telephone.

Not ten seconds later, Orlando appeared in the doorway. "If you please, *signor,*" he said to me, "a trunk call."

My heart suddenly sank.

"Alan? It's me." Terry. "We're in Stra, near Padua. What a place!"

"What's wrong?"

"Not much, just a wheel bearing on the lead truck, but they have to send to Mestre for parts. We'll be a little late."

Oh, Christ. "How late?"

"Better figure four o'clock."

"Terry, listen. We've got a real problem." I filled him in on what was happening.

"Jesus," he said, "the poor kid. I'll do whatever. But a bearing is a bearing, you know?"

"I know. Do the best you can. We'll have to hold the Fishers off somehow."

As I hung up, another horrible thought occurred to me. We had to get the wine out of the trucks and into the count's tanks without the Fishers finding out. That was going to take another couple of hours. To play it safe, we had to stall good old Ellie and Frank until seven o'clock, three hours beyond their deadline.

The count was back in the room when I rejoined the others. "Frank Fisher doesn't want to meet us at the winery at three o'clock," he said. "He wants us to come first to his villa so that we can all go to the winery together. He will give us until four o'clock, as he said. That will be enough time, won't it?"

"Unfortunately not," I said.

Jackie was the first to catch on. "Was that Terry on the phone? What's wrong?"

I explained.

"But that means—"

Ralph cut in to complete the thought. "It means that the wine won't be there on time and those Fishers will get unhappy and do bad things to Sabrina."

"Unless we do something," Jackie said.

"Unless we do something."

"Anybody got any ideas?" I said.

"Yeah," said David. "We get this helicopter—"

"David, be serious," said Jackie.

"Well, how else are we going to get up to this villa without being spotted?"

"Excuse me," said the count, "you will not be able to reach the Fishers' villa unnoticed. They will be watching."

"How about calling Commissario Ratner?" Jackie asked.

"On what pretext? No crime is being committed."

"Your friend Garcia," I said.

"His trucks are being filled now," the count said. "His crew has been working since eight o'clock."

Too late to give the Fishers the count's wine and Garcia the wine from Bled. But still . . .

"He is the father of a daughter," I said.

"True," said Count Emilio. "Garcia would be outraged at an incident of this sort taking place in his . . . in his . . ."

"Turf," David said.

" 'Turf,' exactly. And he would help. But if we tell him about the Fishers, we will have to tell him everything, about the false dealing in wine and the Yugoslav purchase. It will finish me in the wine trade.

"I will do it," the count said, "to save that child from harm. But isn't there some other way?"

"It's simple," I said with a cheeriness I certainly wasn't feeling. "We'll have to rescue Sabrina."

"Who doesn't even know she needs rescuing," said Ralph.

For a long moment, nobody said anything.

I walked over to where we'd set up for rehearsal and mechanically began putting away my instruments and music. An idea was bumping around in my head like a bumble bee in a solarium. But I was so tired that I almost couldn't let it out.

Finally, I went back to Count Emilio. "Wine," I said solemnly.

The count's eyebrows went up. "Wine?"

"The Fishers—will they want, you know, samples of their wine?"

"They have already had them."

"Oh," I said. "Well, we'll bring them some more. You're giving them a few hundred liters of something a little different, you want them to try it before it's loaded. You want to acquaint them with a special bottling for their next time. Who cares?"

"I don't understand," the count said.

"Please," I said. "Just get us inside their villa with a couple of bottles of *something*. One of the bottles has to be wine."

"Ah!" said the count, a sudden gleam in his eye.

"The other bottle—"

"The other bottle has to be a disturbance. Not too little and not too big. If it's too big, the Fishers will shoot, and we don't want shooting."

"Alan French," said Jackie, "don't you dare."

"I will talk with Orlando," said the count. "We did a number of things like this when we were children together. In the war."

"Jackie," I said, "show me another way to get Sabrina out of there. Any other way."

"I don't want you where there's shooting," she said.

"We both don't," I said. "I'll be under the piano, believe me."

"I'll look after him for you," Ralph said.

"Oh, fine!" Jackie's face flushed. "Then *both* of you will get killed. Dammit . . ." When Jackie swore, things were serious. "How do we get *into* these messes?"

"Kismet," said Ralph.

"Fate," said David.

"Karma," I said.

"Shut *up!*" Jackie exploded. "The three of you! Boy warriors, every one! Well, make room in the long house."

"What's that supposed to mean?" I said.

"It's supposed to mean I'm coming with you."

"Oh, no," I said.

"Don't oh-no me . . ."

Before the skirmish could turn into a full-scale war, Count Emilio came back into the room. With him was a beaming Orlando. Cradled against the count's chest were two dusty, cobwebby bottles. Orlando bore a tray on which were half a dozen glasses.

"Are those—?"

"Very good wine, the best of my house," the count said. "One we will drink now." Ceremoniously, he uncorked, poured and handed around the glasses filled with deep red wine.

The wine was wonderful.

"A second glass for each," said the count, "and then the empty bottle to Orlando."

Orlando took the empty and disappeared.

"What's he going to do?" Jackie asked.

"Trust me, my dear Jackie," said the count, "and when the time comes, do exactly as I say."

"But what—?"

"You must come with us," the count said. "It is absolutely essential. The Fishers are suspicious, but they will be less suspicious if you, a woman, are there. Alan, you of course will be the third person. You," he said to Ralph and David, "are reserves. Later, I will tell you what I wish you to do.

"Don't look at me," I said to the two of them. "The count is running this operation."

"I will phone now," said the count.

The count's blue Mercedes swallowed us all easily. With Orlando at the wheel, it took us smoothly and quietly through the old city and out the Via Goffredo Mameli to the Adige and the Statale north.

My stomach was glad Orlando was driving.

"What did you say to the Fishers?" I asked the count, more to cover my nervousness than because I really wanted to know.

"Oh, it was easy," he said. "I said that even if they were very angry about the delay, it would be unnecessary to do anything rash, as the wine would certainly be ready by three o'clock. Then I said that it was a shame to waste a lovely afternoon. I wanted to show you and Jackie the countryside around Caprino, and it would be advantageous for them to have you near. Besides, I had a wine I wished them to try . . ."

"And they swallowed all of that?"

"Why not? The Fishers will use violence if necessary, but they are professionals. Their interest is in the wine. The people they represent, I don't know them, but they are professionals, too. They have put up money. They expect the Fishers to protect their investment, and that is what the Fishers are doing." The count leaned back in his seat. Of all of us, he was the most relaxed. "Now, please listen. The Fishers' villa is a beautiful one, but it is not very large. Do everything you can to find where they have placed the young lady. If the Fishers have her with them, so much the better. But if not, you must locate her.

"When we open the second bottle of wine, there will be a *big* diversion. Pay no attention to anything else, but go to Sabrina and get out of the villa. The drive leading from the villa to the road is a long one, you will see. Leave this car behind and run down it. Another car will be parked at the bottom. You remember Mauro? He will be driving. You and Jackie get in the car with Sabrina and Mauro will drive you to the winery. Wait for us there. Send Sabrina back to Verona with Mauro if you wish."

"What about us?" Ralph asked.

"When you see the others leave, get out of the car and make noise. But stay outside in the gardens. Even if you hear gunfire, which I doubt, do not come inside.

"Eventually, I will come out and Orlando will drive us away."

"Simple as that, eh?" Ralph said.

"Yes," said the count. "The Fishers, as I said, are professionals. As soon as they realize that their hostage is gone, they will adjust to the new reality."

"I hope you're right," I said.

"I hope so, too," said the count.

A few minutes later, we drove through Sant'Ambrogio. I recognized the count's winery. The one glimpse of it from the car window brought back an image, ugly and sharp, of what I'd seen there—could it have been only eight days ago?—Attilio's body in the wine vat. I suddenly felt a huge distaste for what we were about to do. It wasn't so much being scared, although I must admit I *was* scared. It was more a matter of having had an overdose of scheming, deception and violence and of wanting to be purged of it.

"What I'd really like to do," I said to Jackie, squeezing her hand, "is to jump out of this car with you and go sit in the sun in the Erbe and drink white wine."

"You should have thought of that before," she said tartly. But at least she squeezed back.

When the musician has finished . . .
you should quietly return [your damsel]
from the place from whence you led her forth.

Arbeau,
Orchesographie

CHAPTER EIGHTEEN

Beyond Sant'Ambrogio, the road climbed steadily into the uplands of Valpolicella to the west of Lago di Garda. As we neared Caprino, the immense ridge of Monte Baldo began to fill the horizon to the north.

We said nothing as the car swung left and bore us upward away from the town through dark alleys of cypresses. On either side were the gates and driveways of villas set in elaborate gardens. The landscape was lush, manicured and empty of humanity. I would have loved to see even one old man on a creaky bicycle. But nobody was around.

"Gosh, Toto," said Jackie.

We all laughed nervously.

All at once, we were out of the shade and in a world of bright sunlight, on the lip of a bowl scooped out of the southern base of Monte Baldo. The bowl was far from empty. There were turn-offs every few yards. Some led to A-frame and chalet colonies visible from the main road. The one we took was different. It climbed a long slope, then passed between ornamented gates into a parklike enclave. It looked as if the owner of an ancient villa had warded off poverty by carving his immense grounds into vacation estates for a select few of the haves of this world, including the Fishers.

We rounded a curve and swung into a driveway and, far sooner than I wanted, we were there.

Some small birds, chirping distractedly, were hopping around on the gravel. The reason for their agitation was obvious.

Through an open window on the second floor poured forth a flood of sound. Sabrina was doing Madame Klagenhafer's thing. "At least we won't have to wonder where she is," I said to Jackie under my breath.

Ellie Fisher in white crushproof linen and Frank in a silk sports jacket greeted us under the portico of the villa. They didn't look terribly pleased to see us, but then they didn't look terribly displeased, either.

Jackie and I ooh'd and aah'd our way into the drawing room, to the Fishers' self-deprecatory obbligato.

"The kids are grown," Frank Fisher said, "and I'm getting pretty close to retirement. We looked around for ages, and we finally decided this was *the* place. I can keep in touch with my interests from here, and Ellie has the house and her garden."

"Oh, Frank, you make it sound just like Montclair," Ellie Fisher said. "The fact is, it's just the most beautiful place in the world. And so safe! We have our own security force, you know, right on the grounds. When Frank's away, I don't have to worry at all."

I couldn't tell whether Ellie was simply playing upper-class wifey or warning us obliquely not to try anything tricky. In any event, it didn't matter. For the next fifteen minutes, the Fishers took us on a tour of their house and the garden. To give them credit, they had created a paradise, from the dining room with its honey-colored paneling and carved-plaster ceiling to the terrace at the rear of the house, torchlit for al fresco dining, that looked out over olive groves and vineyards toward Monte Baldo.

We came back in and resettled ourselves in what Frank Fisher insisted on calling the front parlor.

"Let me ask you something," he said to the count. " Do you think it might be a good idea to phone up the winery, just to see if anything's going on?" His voice was very polite, but it was still an order.

"I will call, in one minute," the count said. "But I promised you something, and first I'd like to keep the promise."

"Oh," said Ellie Fisher, "the wine."

"Okay," Frank Fisher said, "first we'll try the wine."

Ellie Fisher rang a little bell. When nobody came after a few seconds, she rang louder. "Damn that Egidio," she said. "He thinks just because it's Sunday . . ."

An elderly manservant stepped quietly into the room. It was impossible to tell whether or not he'd overheard.

"Oh, Egidio," Ellie Fisher went on sweetly. She spoke Italian, but with the heaviest possible American accent. I assumed she was asking for glasses and a corkscrew, because that's what Egidio brought in on his tray a few seconds later.

"Allow me," said the count gallantly. He opened the good bottle and handed around glasses, and we all sipped appreciatively.

"That's a lot better than the stuff you're supposed to be shipping me," Frank Fisher barked in his executive voice. "Anybody else want seconds?"

"It's delicious, Emilio," Ellie Fisher said. "Don't you think so, Mr. French?"

"Indeed I do," I said, like the connoisseur I wasn't. Jackie threw me a satiric look, but I was too edgy to respond.

"I think we must have the second bottle," the count said.

"I'd just as soon wait, if it's all the same to you," Frank Fisher said, putting down his glass.

"Now, Frank, you're not being polite," said Ellie Fisher. Her thin face was slightly flushed, and there were tiny beads of perspiration at her hairline. Could Ellie be the least little bit pie-eyed on wine? "I think our guests would enjoy another glass," she said. "I know I would."

"All right. But then I want the count to call his damn winery," Frank Fisher said gruffly.

Delicately, the count eased the cork out of the neck of the second bottle. For a second, nothing happened. I felt disappointed and relieved all at once, the way I felt when I was eleven and my best Fourth of July firecracker just sat there fizzling on the sidewalk: it didn't bang, but it didn't blow my hand off, either.

After that one second, I wasn't disappointed anymore.

There was an ear-shattering roar. Ellie Fisher's face went

white and distorted. Frank Fisher leaped at the count, who jumped nimbly back out of the way and dropped the bottle at Fisher's feet. The bottle was already beginning to spew thick black smoke.

Fisher was yelling, but I was deafened by the explosion and I could only guess what. Besides, something was tugging hard at my arm. I turned to free myself, and it was Jackie, pulling me toward the hall and the elegantly curved stairway to the second floor.

On the way out of the room behind her, I cannoned into Egidio, knocking him down. I distinctly remember stopping to help him to his feet, even as more smoke swirled out of the drawing room behind us. And though I won't swear to it, I think I remember that he was smiling.

I sprinted upstairs. Jackie had already thrown open the double doors of the front room. It too was paneled and elaborately furnished. Its centerpiece was a small Steinway grand, the top a parking place for photos of handsome Fisher children.

Sabrina, her mouth open, stood in the middle of the carpeted floor.

"Come on!" I yelled to her. "Time to go!"

"But . . . Mr. and Mizis Fisher told me to wait."

"No way, let's go!"

Sabrina's face set mulishly.

"Sabrina," Jackie said, "There's a fire downstairs. We have to hurry!"

"Well, I don't see why—"

God must have given me the strength to do it, because otherwise there is no way I could have picked up five-foot-seven-or-so Sabrina, slung her bodily over one shoulder and carried her down that staircase and through the front door.

Luckily, just when I set her on her feet a second loud bang came from the direction of the house and something buzzed angrily by overhead.

"My goodness!" Sabrina squeaked. "Somebody in there's shootin' at us!"

"Run!" I gasped, and the three of us ran.

At the foot of the drive, Mauro was ready. In fact, he had the rear door of his car wide open, and he was tapping the accelerator with his foot. Even before I could slam the door shut, he was roaring out of there in high gear.

There was no need for speed, though, because no one was chasing us. After the first quarter of a mile, our getaway turned into something much more like a Sunday drive with Grandpa in the country.

"Now, Alan, you just have to tell me what in *the* hell was going on back there." The accents of Forest City were very much back in evidence in Sabrina's voice. I devoutly hoped the experiences of the day hadn't scared the Italian out of her.

"Sabrina, when you weren't at rehearsal, we missed you," Jackie was saying.

"Well, I did leave y'all a note," Sabrina said. "At least, I *wrote* a note to say Mr. and Mizis Fisher had invited me up to their villa. For a picnic, you know? We never did have one. And I did think it was sort of funny when they showed me up to that room and then . . . went away. It's a real nice room, and they have a real good piano. But it was *rude*, just leaving me like that. Why, I didn't know how in the world I was going to get back in time."

In time for what? I wondered. And then it hit me. In a few hours, we were supposed to be onstage in Verona, giving a concert.

"Sabrina, don't be upset about it," I said. "The Fishers are in business with Count Emilio, buying and selling wine. And something went wrong. We were just scared that you might get caught in the middle."

"Something went wrong? You mean, like the moonshining back home?"

What a happy thought. "Like that," I said.

"Well!" Sabrina said. "I don't want any part of it, then. Those moonshiners are terrible. People think they're romantic, but they're just hoody."

"I don't think the count's like that," said Jackie.

"I don't care, I'm real glad y'all came and got me. Even if you did practically squeeze me in half bringing me downstairs."

The trip to Sant'Ambrogio was peacefully anticlimactic. True to the count's plan, Mauro dropped Jackie and me at the winery, then drove off to Verona with Sabrina.

"Don't y'all be late," she called as the car pulled away.

Jackie and I walked up to the winery entrance. It was locked. I rattled the door, then tried banging on it, but nobody came.

"There must be *somebody* around," I said. "I'll go have a look around."

"You will not!" Jackie said. "You stay right here. And you put your arms around me and hold me." Even in the heat of the early afternoon, she shivered. "Otherwise, I'm going to sit down right here on these steps and burst into tears."

"Let's both sit down," I said.

We were still sitting there fifteen minutes later when the convoy of wine tankers from Bled rolled up, shattering the Sunday-afternoon silence, and Terry Monza climbed grinning from the cab of the lead truck.

"Boy, are we ever glad to see you!" I said.

Terry was sweaty and rumpled and badly in need of a shave, but Jackie jumped up and gave him a big hug anyway.

"I dunno," Terry said. "What you have to do to earn ninety big ones, it's pretty rough."

"Ninety big ones less shipping," I said.

"Shipping is only about seven thousand bucks."

"Only," I said.

"Yeah, but do those guys ever earn their dough." Terry told us about driving overloaded tankers over the mountains from Bled to the border at night. "You can see the skid marks where other trucks have gone over, and you wonder if your turn is coming up."

Then he went on about Stra, a village halfway to nowhere, and about finding out at 6 A.M. that one of the tankers had a cracked wheel bearing. "The whole village is Commie, thank God," he said, and only too eager to do the Yugoslavs a favor, which is how they got one of the locals to ride his motorbike all

the way to Mestre on a Sunday, open up his cousin's parts warehouse and bring back a new bearing.

Terry was just waxing eloquent on the mechanical details of
how to change a wheel bearing when the door to the winery
opened behind us. Milos, the head tanker driver, had had the
sense to do what Jackie and I had been too shaken to do: go
around to the yard behind the building and pound on the gate.
The winery work crew was there waiting for the trucks to ar-
rive. They were perfectly happy to let us in—and get a good
look at Jackie—and then leave us to ourselves in the offices.

I was the one closest to the telephone when it rang, so I
picked up the receiver. "Hello . . . I mean *Pronto.*"

"Never mind what you mean, you sorry sonofabitch," Frank
Fisher's voice rasped sourly in my ear. "Where the hell is my
wine?"

"Right in the winery where it should be," I said ambiguously,
"and it wouldn't hurt you to be a little more polite."

"Yeah, well, I don't need lessons in manners from you,"
Fisher said. "Coming in here with a smoke bomb like that. You
scared poor Ellie practically out of her mind with that thing,
and the whole place is a mess."

"Gee, that's too bad," I said. "If you hadn't abducted poor
little Sabrina—"

"What do you mean, abducted? She was here as our guest."

"She didn't feel much like a guest when someone took a shot
at us going down the drive."

"That was Ellie."

"*Ellie?*"

Fisher's voice was sheepish. "She was very upset, she thought
the whole house was being firebombed. So she grabbed a gun I
have . . . but she's never hit a target in her life."

I suddenly had an inspiration. "Maybe not, Fisher, though
Sabrina Englander still doesn't think much of your hospitality.
But she might not say anything about being kidnapped if we can
sort out this wine deal in a friendly way."

There was a silence. It was my impression that Fisher was
thinking at some length about what charges of kidnapping and

assault with a deadly weapon would do to his and Ellie's local reputation.

"Maybe it was kind of a dumb idea to bring the little gal up here," he said. "You think you can handle it?"

"Try me," I said. "You be here at seven and we'll have a warehouse receipt all ready for you."

"I guess that's fair enough," Fisher said grudgingly.

"See you at seven, then," I said and hung up.

"Very impressive," Terry said.

"You really are clever when you want to be," said Jackie.

"Thanks, fans," I said. "Now let's figure out a way to get into Verona. I still want to hear What's-it do her songs."

Dancing, or saltation, is both a pleasant
and a profitable art.

Arbeau,
Orchesographie

CHAPTER NINETEEN

Getting back to Verona was easy. Minutes after my talk with
Fisher, Count Emilio's blue Mercedes drew up in front of the
winery, with everybody inside intact. The count strode in, calling for his foreman. He stayed long enough to be sure that the
unloading was going smoothly, bundled Jackie, Terry and me
into the car with Ralph, David and Orlando and took the wheel
himself.

"Our expedition was a glorious success!" he said gleefully.

The Fishers, once they'd realized that Sabrina was out of their
reach, had behaved like the realists they were. The one gunshot
was the only bit of violence. Both had fussed loudly about the
damage to their villa, but they'd calmed down when they'd realized that most of the damage was superficial. In fact, the count
said, they had even apologized for carrying off Sabrina and cre-
ating a problem where none had existed.

"That's it," said Terry. "Why would smart people like the
Fishers want leverage they don't need?"

"Who knows?" said Count Emilio, somehow shrugging and
negotiating a turn at the same time.

I had some ideas on that score, but I kept them to myself.

"Listen," I said to the count. "I want to be the person who
hands the warehouse receipt to Frank Fisher."

"But we have a concert," Jackie protested.

"At eight-thirty," I said. "I'll be finished with Fisher by
seven-thirty."

The count glanced over at me curiously.

"Humor me," I said.

"Mauro will drive you and wait for you," said the count.

"Perfect," I said. "That solves the problem."

"Is it safe?" Jackie asked anxiously.

The count, cutting into the wrong lane, narrowly missed a BMW. "Oh, yes, I think so. Why not? Frank Fisher wants his wine, Alan French gives him his wine, goodbye."

"Want any of us to come with you?" asked Ralph.

"Nope. I just want to get this deal done."

"Good," said the count. "Then tomorrow morning we will meet right after breakfast and settle our accounts."

When we got back to the palazzo, I made everybody sit in on the run-through of Sabrina's Monteverdi songs, partly to elicit comment and partly to get our collective minds back on music.

Afterward, Jackie and I climbed the stairs to our room, closed the shutters and stretched out on the big bed.

Jackie yawned. "You know what I want?"

"No, what?"

"I want a heavy ball and a large iron chain. To tie to your leg."

"So I won't get in trouble, you mean."

"Exactly."

"Jackie . . ." There was nothing I wanted to do more than lie there with her and drowse and be in love.

"Whatever sweet talk you have in mind, forget it," she said.

"Jackie . . ."

"I don't want to hear about it."

I reached over and undid the third button of her blouse.

Immediately, she flopped over on her stomach and tucked both hands protectively under her. "No you don't," she said, her voice muffled by the pillow.

I put a hand on her back and rubbed gently at the base of her spine.

"Mmmm," she said. "That feels great. Men are beasts. You are a man. Therefore . . ."

I kept on rubbing. "I'll be back in time."

"You probably will," Jackie said, rolling over again and sitting up. "You have a nasty habit of showing up at the very, very last second and doing just beautifully. But you also have a nasty habit of first going off by yourself and driving everybody crazy. Don't you think it's about time you kicked your habit?"

It was the kind of remark that you need forty-five minutes to answer, while your relationship hangs precariously in the balance, and I didn't have forty-five minutes.

"Yes," I said, "it is time. But I don't know if I can do it."

"Try," she said. "Try hard, because it's getting late and I don't think it's funny. Or brave."

I reached for her then, and we sat awkwardly in the middle of the bed while she buried her face in my shoulder and gave a couple of hard, dry sobs.

"I love you," I said. "You know that."

"You'd better," she said. "Because otherwise we're using up a lot of energy for nothing. Now, let's get up. I want to put some cold water on my face and take a bath and wash my hair and you've got to get going."

I washed my own face and got.

Milos the head trucker was waiting for me in the office so he could get a receipt and take off. When the shipping bill came, the bank would pay it. Fisher drove up a few minutes later. I got wearily to my feet and went to meet him. He was still wearing his silk sports jacket. I wondered vaguely why it wasn't sooty from the smoke bomb, but it wasn't.

"Okay," I said. "This thing is a metric measuring stick. You use it—"

"I know what you use it for," he said quickly.

"Fine. Let's just go down the line and stick every tank so you can be sure you're getting what you're paying for."

He followed me down the corridor and into the storage chamber. I flicked on the lights. Stick in hand, he climbed the stairs to the catwalk and began the routine of inserting the stick in the filler pipe of each tank. There were a couple of dozen tanks, and after he'd done a few he got bored, but he kept on going to the end.

"All right," he said, coming back down to floor level. "I'm satisfied." He handed back the stick. "I'll take my receipt."

"Fisher," I said, "who killed Attilio Caspardino?"

"The receipt," he repeated. He put menace into his voice, but his pleasant looks and party clothes made it seem like an act. I took the receipt out of my pocket and held it so he could see it. "In a minute."

"I'm not saying anything," Fisher said angrily, "but I'll tell you this. Attilio was a shit. A real little bastard."

"That's what everybody says," I agreed.

"You know what the little bastard was trying to do?" Fisher's face darkened at the recollection. "He was telling me that Emilio was out of wine! Emilio! I've done business with Emilio Sabinetti for years, never had a problem until this year. All of a sudden, I get a call up at the villa. Attilio. Please, *signor*, can I come see you, very important. So I say, Sure, and up he comes and tells me his cousin is cheating on me. On me! Goddammit, French or whatever your name is, do you know who I represent?"

"I've got a fair idea," I said.

"Well, Emilio knows. And Emilio doesn't cheat. He sells me good wine, whatever I want, I get it back to the States and do what I want with it. I can put Emilio's wine in the best clubs, people lap it up like—" All of a sudden, Fisher cut himself short. His eyes grew wary, as if he'd said too much already. "Anyway, there's a lot of pressure in this business. Attilio . . . what happened to him, it's a terrible thing to say, but he had it coming.

"Now, give me my receipt and let me get the hell out of here."

"So that's why you grabbed Sabrina," I said. "You were afraid Attilio might be right and the count might be out of wine."

"Well, Attilio was wrong," said Fisher. "And if I can give you a piece of friendly advice, this is a very easy business to be wrong in. You want to be careful what you say and who you say it to."

"I don't doubt it," I said. I handed him the receipt.

He read it through, folded it carefully and tucked it into his inside jacket pocket. "My best to Emilio," he said on his way out. "And good luck with your music."

I looked at my watch. Seven-thirty. And I was starving.

"Mauro," I said in the car, "near San Zeno is a *tavola calda*."

"I know the one," he said. "It's not very good."

"I'm sure one of my friends will be there," I said.

Sure enough, David, already in his formal gear, was sitting at the counter, attacking a Veronese pizza and washing it down with one of those strange licorice-flavored soft drinks the Italians love. When he saw me, he stopped eating for the moment. "You made it," he said. "Good deal. Jackie brought your stuff over to the church."

A big bowl of *pastina in brodo* made me feel a lot better. So also did the comforting knowledge that ninety thousand dollars, more or less, was nestling in our bank in Venice. For once, the Antiqua Players could afford to stumble through a recital.

We paid up and started across the piazza to San Zeno.

"Hey," said David, echoing my thoughts. "I just remembered. We're pretty rich, huh?"

"Well . . ."

"Because, look, I really need to do something about these." He pointed to his black shoes.

"You're right," I said. "If jackie gets a look at those . . . What is that stuff, electrician's tape?"

"Yeah. Actually, it holds pretty well. But I figure, they make great shoes in Italy, right?"

"Here, for God's sake," I said. I tore a fifty-dollar traveler's check out of the little folder and signed it over. "We'll take it out of your concert money."

"Thanks, Alan. I'll get them tomorrow."

"I'm the one who's grateful," I said to Jackie a few minutes later.

"I know," she said, looking up from the fret she was retying on the fingerboard of her gamba. "When you're taking care of the big things like David's shoes, the small stuff like wine deals and murder goes a million miles away."

"I love you," I said.

"You did get back early, I must say."

"That proves it," I said.

"You know in the Veracini, measure fifty-three?"

The Veracini was my big number, a sonata for violin and continuo. "What about it?"

"I think you should retard."

"Stop changing the subject," I said.

"Okay, then, I love you, too," she said. She smiled at me.

"I'll retard. Tell Ralph in case I forget."

We've certainly played better technically than we played that evening. The opener, *El Marchese di Saluzzo*, was slaphappy instead of deliberately raucous and the dance suite was uneven. Ralph's Frescobaldi helped redeem the first half of the program, and Sabrina's Monteverdi songs went well, except that yours truly played a rather poor viol part in the song about the fragile violet.

Even so, I've rarely enjoyed an appearance more. For some reason, maybe the acoustics in the old church, the familiar music sounded especially fresh and delightful. The faces of the four others, dimly lit from below, were the faces of people closer to me than my closest kin. I knew their expressions so well: the furrow between Jackie's eyebrows that appeared only when she was playing; Ralph's half smile; the way Terry's shoulders hunched as he leaned into a solo; David's incredibly long fingers. That evening, something sparked in every exchange of glances. Even Sabrina the outsider caught something of our feeling. When her turn came, instead of standing and singing as if she were all alone onstage, she came in close and sang *with* us for the first time.

At intermission, my eyes were wet. And mine weren't the only ones.

"I could hug you all," I said. "Now let's settle down and give them some music."

Half an hour later, I was regretting my words.

Midway through the second half of the program, and just before my Veracini, David plumped his chitarrone on his lap.

A theorbo is a big lute. A chitarrone is a huge theorbo. It's strung with brass, which makes it sound something like a harpsichord. But its strings are plucked by hand, so, unlike a harpsichord, it can be made to whisper or to ring out loudly. A good player can do a lot with the ungainly thing.

That evening, David Brodkey was playing two toccatas and a fugue on the chitarrone. Six bars into the first toccata, I decided to get up and walk out. There was no way I could follow David's act.

What the hell, I shrugged to myself after twelve bars, I might as well stick around. There's no way Heifetz could follow it, either.

David had to take five bows. While the applause was rolling on and on, I had plenty of time to wonder why I hadn't followed in the footsteps of my cousin Ethan. Ethan was an allergist in New Rochelle, New York, and he doesn't have a worry in the world.

Then it was my turn.

Veracini is a less imaginative, more Italianate Handel. He's violinistic, which means that his work teems with jumps and skips and double stops and elaborate ornaments. Those were okay. What wasn't okay is that Veracini, for all of his scrimshaw, is very exposed melodically. Make a mistake and there's no place to hide. Your ineptitude hangs out there for the whole world to hear.

Mine didn't manifest itself until measure eight.

I'd risen to my feet, tucked my fiddle manfully under my chin and nodded to Jackie and Ralph to begin.

With vast satisfaction, I'd heard myself attack the opening allegro, getting the big, swelling sound I fancied.

I can't explain it. We were bouncing along toward a full close in D and I hit it a full, ripe, plummy semitone flat.

Of course, I sharpened it up right away. Terrific. Alan French and his musical saw.

Automatically, I registered Jackie's startled look and Ralph's raised eyebrows. When Sabrina had dried during the *L'Arianna* opening, at least nothing had come out. But this . . .

The only thing you can do is try to make your audience forget your blunder. To do this, you have to forget it yourself. That's far from easy, especially when you're playing from memory and have no printed music to help move your eye and mind ahead. You can try. You can tell yourself, I'll play the *rest* of this music more brilliantly then anyone has ever played it before.

Tell yourself that and, believe me, you're headed straight for another disaster.

I thought about something else.

I thought about ninety thousand dollars.

I thought about Jackie's smile.

I was halfway through the andante second movement before I realized that things were back on track. I was playing well. If I could take the *alla breve* final movement at speed, I could wipe out the evil memory of that D-flat.

As we approached the end of the andante, I waggled my chin at Ralph. Pay attention, my signal was saying. I'm going to take off.

One, two . . .

I was getting the notes fine, and Ralph and Jackie were with me. It was quick but not prestissimo, there was still enough time for some halfway decent phrasing, I had this movement by the short hairs.

Oh, God. I sucked in a breath.

A drop of sweat was rolling down my nose.

I shook my head slightly to dislodge it. No luck.

It hung there as I played. I could imagine it, big and luminous, getting bigger, quivering as I moved. Disgusting. Distracting.

I reached the end of the repeat of the first strain and did some hard bowing to get into the second strain.

My nose began to itch.

Get on with the music.

Gradually, the itch became a burning. The tip of my nose started to smolder. I kept on playing. Then my nose caught fire. I knew who I was. I was Nero, fiddling while my nose burned. The thought made me giggle to myself, and I nearly missed a note.

And then I was finishing the repeat of the second strain and skidding in for a landing, on time and on target. Done.

I stood there, out of breath, smiling. The applause was solid. I bowed to it: once, twice, three times. Then it died down. I took my seat again, sighing with relief. Now, at last, I could scratch . . .

Damned if the itch hadn't gone away.

CHAPTER TWENTY

"Why were you making those awful faces? In your solo."

A cool breeze found its way between the slats of the shutters and ruffled Jackie's dark hair. It was long past midnight, but neither of us was asleep. We'd left the others an hour before, but there was the whole improbable day to recapitulate and the music to reprise, and certain other activities had preoccupied us as well.

I told her why I'd made faces. She laughed and rubbed my nose with a forefinger and kissed it fondly. "It's over, isn't it?" she said.

"All over but the shouting," I said. Alan the prophet, that's me.

"Hey, kid, you guys were pretty good last night, but you better sharpen up on that fiddle. See you later." Manny Gardi came up behind me, put an arm around my shoulder, delivered his verdict and breezed on by. A nice guy.

I shifted my violin case to my left hand and turned down the corridor toward the count's offices. It was early: I had plenty of time to settle up with Count Emilio before I was due at Manny's rehearsal. A nice warm glow of financial anticipation kept me company on my stroll.

The count's antechamber was empty. But the sounds coming from the inner office turned the nice warm glow into an icy chill.

I stepped cautiously nearer and peered inside.

The woman who was screaming had her back to me. From what I could see of her, she was in her late thirties or early forties, and not unattractive, with ash-blond hair in a ponytail. She wore a yellow-and-white-striped dress and earrings, like any of the fashionable Veronese matrons in the shops and cafés along the *Listone* of the Piazza Bra.

The count said something to her. It sounded like, "Please . . . please, Teresa . . ."

She went on at the top of her lungs. I couldn't understand one word in ten. But one of the words I could understand was "Attil-io," and another was "*u-ccide.*" Gradually, it dawned on me who she was and what she was shouting. She was Attilio's widow. And she was accusing the count of Attilio's murder.

She gestured crazily. My stomach churned when I saw that the hand she was waving held a gleaming single-edged chef's knife.

I tiptoed closer, close enough to see the spittle that sprayed from her lips as she shouted. The count saw me and his eyes widened, but she never heard me, not even when I raised my arm and swiped at her fiercely with the only weapon I had at hand.

My violin.

The blow hit her squarely on the knot of her ponytail. She staggered forward, more startled than hurt, and grabbed at the edge of the desk to recover her balance. The count moved like a cat. Before she could pull away, he'd pinned her right hand and forced the fingers back. The knife fell to the floor.

I swung the violin case at her a second time. It was a horrible mistake. This time it fell open. I watched, cringing, as my violin slid out of the case, spun once in the air and thudded to the carpet.

The woman saw it fall. She made an indescribable sound. She might have been laughing. She brought her foot up in front of her and stamped down hard. The violin crumpled like matchwood under her stiletto heel.

I know I cried out. If the count hadn't shoved me aside, I

would have committed murder myself. He was the one who grabbed her and held her while I ran out to the phone.

She was screaming again when the police arrived.

"You know what Teresa Caspardino was saying?" Commissario Ratner demanded. He had come later, after his colleagues had summoned the ambulance and it had driven off with its sedated, restrained passenger. Needless to say, I wouldn't be doing any rehearsing that morning.

I shook my head dully. My violin was in ruins, beyond all hope of restoration. For years it had been part of me, and I was appalled at the loss. I wanted to hear nothing about the demented stranger who had made it happen.

"She was saying that the Americans from Caprino had killed her husband. You know who these Americans are?"

"I assume the Fishers."

"Yes. Do you think the Fishers did kill Caspardino?"

"I have no idea," I said. "For all I know, you killed him."

"You know better than to joke with the police, especially of a foreign country," Ratner said sharply. "We police are not humorists."

"All right," I said. "I know this much. The count's cousin Attilio had been spreading rumors about the count in the local wine trade. He'd made some powerful enemies. Frank Fisher was one of them. So was your friend Reyes Garcia. Probably there were others. You would know who they are."

"What rumors?"

"Rumors that the count had run out of wine. The count will tell you more. He's heard that Attilio went to other vintners to tell them not to sell wine to the count, to hold out for higher prices. He thinks that Attilio was hoping to earn a commission on those sales. But Attilio was greedy. He wanted to see if the count would pay him not to spread such tales. That is why he made the dinner appointment with the count on the day he was killed. The count asked me to come along as a witness."

"And did the count pay?"

"Of course not," I said. "There was no truth to the rumors. The count had ample supplies of wine and was readily able to fill his orders. If Attilio had kept the appointment, the count would have told him so."

"It could be that what you say is true," said Ratner thoughtfully. "It accords with things I have heard from others. But tell me . . . have you no opinion at all as to who did the murder?"

"None, except that it would not have been the count. Why would anybody run the risk of murder to silence rumors that he could prove were false?"

Ratner nodded.

"You know what I think?" I went on, "I think you'll hunt for a long time before you find proof of who killed Attilio Caspardino."

Ratner looked at me consideringly. "I am afraid you are right," he said. "This is a small community, and it knows how to keep its secrets."

"Are we done?" I asked.

"We are never done," he said sententiously. "But, yes, for now you are free. And I thank you for your assistance."

I looked around, but there was no sign of the count, so I left.

Jackie was waiting in the courtyard. Orlando had told her most of what had happened. I put down my violin case with the ruined instrument inside, and sat beside her. It was beautifully quiet and peaceful there, and I felt miserable.

"What do I do now?" I said.

"That's easy," she said. "First, we rent you a violin from somebody in town and we finish the festival. Next, we go to Yugoslavia for a week."

"Yugoslavia?"

"It's so beautiful, and Vivi and Petar have invited us, and I want to go."

"Okay," I said, "Yugoslavia."

"Just for a week. And then . . ."

"And then?" I prompted.

"We go home and get married."

"We do what?" Suddenly, I began to feel a lot less miserable.

"Don't you want to?"

"I—"

"You don't have to marry me if you don't want to."

"I—"

"I'll understand."

"Rich lady," I said dazedly, "you just found yourself a husband."

"It's now or never," Jackie said, "and that means now."

We told the others right away. The prevailing opinion, expressed politely but firmly by Ralph, was that it was none too soon. Then we went for a walk, and got back just in time to eat a bite, change and catch the bus to San Zeno for *L'Arianna*. Sabrina sang flawlessly. I played a borrowed violin and lived through it. We're professionals, you understand, cool and imperturbable. But every time I looked over at Jackie that evening, I grinned most unprofessionally from ear to ear.

"I have to go see him," I said to her after breakfast the next morning. "He owes us money."

"He does indeed," said a deep voice behind me. "And more besides." Count Emilio put an arm around each of us and walked us to his office. "First, business." The document he handed me was a bank statement. It showed a credit balance after withdrawals of fourteen billion eight hundred twelve million lire. At the current rate, this came to eighty-nine thousand seven hundred sixteen dollars and thirteen cents.

I showed it to Jackie.

"Ours?" she asked.

"Yours," said the count. "Now, pleasure. To you, my dear friend," he said with a smile, "my heartiest congratulations. And to you"—he held Jackie's hand gently, then brought it to his lips with incomparable finesse—"much, much happiness."

"Emilio," Jackie said. "If Alan runs away, will you marry me?"

"Alas!" said the count. "He will not run away."

"I'm afraid not," I said.

"One more thing," the count said. "It's embarrassing. But yesterday . . . that unfortunate woman . . . the police . . . you know, you saved my life. Not to mention my honor."

It *was* embarrassing. "Please," I said.

"I will say no more," said the count. "But . . . take this." He thrust a bulky, oddly shaped brown paper parcel into my hands. "Open it," he commanded.

It was a violin case. My heart began to beat faster.

"Open it," the count said again.

I flicked the catches and swung the lid upward.

The violin lay in a bed of faded, padded red silk velvet. Belly and ribs were a glowing brown gold: pine and pearwood, beautifully matched. A master maker's product, and old.

"May I?" I asked.

"Of course."

I slipped the instrument free and held it in my right hand.

"Oh, my," said Jackie.

"Tune it," said the count. "Try it."

The strings, too, were old. I tested them gingerly and tuned them low. The bow in the case was a good one, almost a match for the violin. "It needs rosin," I said.

"Of course, of course. Try it!"

As I slipped the instrument under my chin, I felt a pang of disloyalty and regret for my own broken fiddle. But there is no way to say what I felt when I first touched the strings of this one with the bow and heard it speak, at first hesitantly, then with fuller voice.

"You like it?" asked the count.

"It's glorious," I said.

"It is yours."

I lowered the violin and bow and stood staring at him. "No," I said.

"I insist. It is a fine instrument. A Rogeri."

I nodded.

"It has been in our family for two centuries. After the war, we had it restored in Brescia, where it was made. Now you must take it. It should be played."

"Sure," I said, "but by a Stern or a Zuckerman, not by a French."

"And why not?"

"I'm a journeyman. This is a fiddle for a genius."

"Maybe it will make you into a genius. And if not, what then? A violin is meant to be used. If you don't play this one, it will stay in a glass case in my home forever. What a waste!"

"I'd be afraid," I said.

"Be afraid, then. I give it to you. It's your wedding present. How can you be afraid of a wedding present?"

"Jackie," I said desperately.

"In our family, the husband makes the big decisions," she said demurely.

I drew a deep, deep breath. "Okay. I accept. I can't thank you. I won't even try. But . . . let me restring it and tune it and play it for you. If I disgrace it, I'll give it back."

The count smiled. "Good. When can I hear it?"

"Tomorrow," I said. "We'll come at dusk and play Corelli for you in your garden."

"Wonderful," Count Emilio said. "And then we will drink wine!"

We did it, too.

Quartet  Qrime